PRAISE FOR

"I wanted a book about smart and competent people that was low on the angst and would leave me smiling. I'm happy to report that I got exactly what I wanted, and I'd like more of it, please and thank you."

~ Shannon C., The Good, The Bad, and The Unread

"This is a great debut story from Alexa Rowan and I can't wait for more from her."

~ Mary Mooney, Wicked Reads

"You know when you just want something light and sexy, without too much angst? Well this would definitely hit the spot. It has some lovely humour, some very thoughtful moments and plenty of sexiness.... In this well written story it is easy to just keep turning the pages to find out just how Ms. Rowan can make things work - something she does with style."

~ Ruthie Taylor, Wicked Reads

"A perfectly lovely debut contemporary romance from Alexa Rowan.... Great catnip for those who like a good grovel!"

~ Elisabeth Lane, Cooking Up Romance

"Winning Her Over was a very charming and insightful debut, and I would be happy to read more Alexa Rowan in the future."

~ Ana Coqui, Immersed In Books

"If you're looking for a good contemporary, with strong and believable characters and a hero who knows how to grovel properly, you're in for a treat."

~ Gisele, Gisele Reads

Cheryl,
Happy reading!
xo,
Alexa Rowan

WINNING
HER OVER

A BigLaw Romance Novel

ALEXA ROWAN

JASMINE
PRESS.

Published by Jasmine Press
P.O. Box 750005
Arlington Heights, MA 02475
www.jasminepress.com

JASMINE
PRESS

Print Edition 1.1
ISBN: 978-1-942802-01-3

You can find Alexa on the web at www.alexarowan.com!

*For my husband, who always
sees right to the heart of the matter.*

ACKNOWLEDGEMENTS

Winning Her Over would not be the book it is today without the emotional support and writing assistance of my invaluable critique partners, London Setterby, Isley Robson, and Delia Devry. I am likewise tremendously grateful to my editors, Jessa Slade and Martha Trachtenberg.

Thank you to my rock-star beta readers, Martin, Aimee, Diane, and Jessica. Special thanks to massage therapists J.T., and Linda Guttman, LMT, for keeping me on the straight and narrow. All errors are, of course, my own.

Gina Bernal's feedback on the original version of *Winning Her Over* was incredibly helpful in shifting the course of this book. And Serena Bell, your encouragement, especially in the early days, means more to me than I can say.

Can't forget a shout out to the Dragonflies! I'm so lucky that you've got my back, and I will always have yours. You ladies are amazing, every single one of you.

Last, but certainly not least, I can't thank my family enough for your understanding and support. I heart you guys, with all the hearts in the world.

1

LIKE A HEAVILY LADEN PACK MULE, Brenna Nakamura plodded down one of the long corridors of the Rajah Hotel, her footsteps muffled by the plush carpet. Her portable massage table and oversized duffel bag swung in counterpoint to each step of her slow, rolling gait.

Ah, there it was. Room 619 had a choice location near the end of the hall, on the side with a view of the Boston Public Garden's spring magnificence. She checked the hotel's folio, confirming her client's name: Calvin Wilcox.

The man inside that hotel room—most likely a paunchy, middle-aged businessman, in her experience—represented one step closer to financial solvency. For this month, at any rate.

At some point, she'd accept the inevitable and give up her dream. But if Serenity Massage closed its doors, then she'd have to admit that Gregory, her ex-boyfriend, had been right. Her shrinking bank balance was certainly damning evidence that leaving management consulting for massage therapy five years ago was... What had he called it? Oh, now she remembered. The most jaw-droppingly idiotic idea he'd ever heard.

Eh, who was she kidding. Try though she might to forget his harsh words, they still resounded with nauseating clarity every time she "borrowed" a little more from her rainy day fund.

Gregory hadn't been content with trashing her career plans, either. Dumping her immediately afterward had been his jerkhole-flavored icing on the cake. She couldn't entirely blame him for kicking her out of their shared apartment, though—after all, his parents had owned the place, and they'd never hidden their disdain for her.

She realized she'd been staring at the room number on her client's door and exhaled a long, shuddery breath. These negative memories of the past weren't going to help her achieve her vision of the future.

And she wasn't going to give up her entrepreneurial ambitions without a fight. So no matter how tired she was as the end of this interminable day approached, no matter how worried she was about her precarious financial situation, she would damn well be wearing a smile when her client opened the door.

She straightened the loose ponytail gathered at her neck. Then she tapped on the thick wooden door. "Mr. Wilcox? It's Brenna, from Serenity Massage."

"Hang on," a husky baritone replied, accompanied by the muffled thud of footsteps approaching her.

Pasting on a friendly expression, she stepped back as the door swung inward. Only to be confronted by a broad expanse of chest, not quite encased in one of the hotel's signature white terry robes. Her gaze rose to the sturdy column of her client's neck before stalling out at his face, half a foot above her own.

Her jaw slackened as her expectations valiantly tried to catch up to reality. If she'd had a checklist for Male

Aesthetic Perfection, this guy would have ticked every box, from his athletic build to his chiseled jaw and slanting cheekbones. A smattering of freckles across the bridge of his nose saved him—barely—from being intimidatingly gorgeous. But his lips were flattened with tension, and his damp, sandy blond hair looked rumpled, as if he'd just run a hand through it.

Brenna could recognize a fellow stressed-out human being when she saw one, and that brought her back to the reason she was there. "Hi," she said, hoping he didn't notice how breathless she sounded.

"Please, come in." The rumble of his voice slid over her like warm honey.

He backed a few steps into the room's foyer before leading her into the sitting area, which boasted the Rajah's trademark opulence. Rich fabrics and leather impeccably complemented the modern mahogany furniture. The heavy drapes were already drawn across the floor-to-ceiling windows she knew hid behind them.

She set down her massage gear next to the coffee table, then lowered her duffel onto the sofa. Meanwhile, her client stood near the pristine king-sized bed, looking anywhere but at her.

He wasn't the only one who was nervous. Clients as good-looking as he was didn't cross her path often, but they'd never fazed her before. This guy, on the other hand, sent her pulse all thready.

"So, where do you want me?" he asked.

She dug deep for her professionalism and kept her voice low and calm. "It'll take me a few minutes to set up, so you can just make yourself comfortable for now, Mr.

Wilcox."

He sat on the edge of the bed. "Please, call me Cal. Mr. Wilcox makes me think of my dad." His attempt at a grin didn't quite reach his gray eyes, which were pinched at the corners with strain.

She frowned in empathy. "Do you spend a lot of time working on a computer?"

"Way, way more than I'd like," he replied with gritted teeth. Then he began kneading the back of his neck with one of his big, strong hands. "My head is fuh…reaking killing me right now."

His tone piqued her interest, even as his word substitution had her hiding a smile. He sounded a lot like she had, before her career change. "What do you do?"

"I'm an attorney. I'm up here for a trial that starts tomorrow."

"Ah." That explained a lot. "Let me get set up and we'll see what I can do for you."

Brenna shrugged off her belted fleece jacket and laid it across the sofa's arm, next to her duffel. Underneath it, she wore a silky, purplish-gray tunic and matching pants. The wrap-around top was stylish—for a uniform—but for a fleeting moment she wished she'd had the Serenity Massage logo emblazoned on tailored spa dresses instead of the flowing, practical styles she'd chosen.

Not that it mattered what she was wearing, she reminded herself, so long as her appearance was professional. The Rajah Hotel had called her to Cal's room because she was a licensed massage therapist lucky enough to have been added to their referral list. Remaining on that list was far more important than trying to make herself more attractive to one of their guests, no matter how much of a hunk he might be.

Right now, she needed to focus on adjusting the height of the massage table, and on setting her newest client at ease. "Have you had a massage before, Cal?"

"Not a professional one."

Brenna glanced up at him, but he didn't seem to be insinuating anything by the remark. At least, nothing was evident in his facial expression. Though she'd be surprised if a guy as hot as Cal had never gotten a massage from a girlfriend or lover.

She studiously ignored his gaze, as he watched her stand the table upright and cover it with sheets and a lightweight blanket. Sticking to the task at hand, she gave him her new-client spiel.

"When I'm done setting up, I'll step into the bathroom to wash my hands while you disrobe to whatever extent you feel comfortable with. You'll be covered by a drape at all times." She paused, making sure her expression was as neutral as possible. "The less you're wearing, the easier it is for me." *To appreciate your spectacular body.* She gave herself a mental wrist-slap before continuing. "I can work with anything, though."

Frowning, he grunted noncommittally.

Brenna let out the breath she hadn't realized she was holding. "We'll start with you lying on your front, then I'll have you flip over." She inserted a doughnut-shaped face cradle into one end of the table, then lined it with a soft cloth. "There we are."

She turned around, zeroing in on Cal's lips, this time. They looked…rather delectable. She swallowed before meeting his tired eyes. "Any questions?"

He shook his head.

"Is it okay if I turn up the heat? I don't want you to get cold while I'm working on you."

"Yeah, that's fine. Whatever you need."

"Great. I'll knock to let you know I'm coming back in."

She pulled her cosmetics bag out of one of the duffel's outer pockets. Then she adjusted the thermostat by a few degrees, turned down the lights, and escaped into Cal's bathroom, shutting the door behind her.

Away from his compelling presence, she grew less flustered. After three long years with little time for anything except keeping Serenity Massage afloat, she could be forgiven for finding him appealing. Couldn't she?

The humid air was scented with a pleasant soapy fragrance, and droplets still clung to the sides of the glass shower recess. A towel was spread out on the heated rack. *Do* not *imagine your hot client in the shower!*

Instead, she rummaged in her cosmetics bag until she found what she was looking for—lip gloss. Being mostly a non–makeup-wearing kind of girl, it was the best she could do under the circumstances.

She unscrewed the cap and faced her reflection in the mirror, lip gloss at the ready. Then she straightened, looking herself in the eye. Her lips were fine the way they were. She was there to do her job, not doll herself up. She put the lip gloss away, unused.

Brenna washed and dried her hands before folding a couple of clean hotel towels across her arm. Inhaling deeply, she turned back to the door. Showtime.

She knocked twice, then opened the door a crack.

"Cal? Are you ready?"

"As I'll ever be," he quipped.

She pulled the door all the way open, illuminating Cal's tousled hair and powerful shoulders. The rest of his body was outlined underneath the sheet and blanket, which now hung askew.

Ignoring the temptation to ogle her client, she stepped through the doorway. Then she shut the door behind her, returning the bedroom to its dimly lit state.

She tucked her cosmetics bag back into its duffel pocket and laid the towels on the coffee table, within easy reach. All that remained was to dig out her pump-bottle of massage oil and its nylon holster from the nearly empty duffel, and strap the holster around her hips.

After sliding a pillow under Cal's shins, she adjusted the covers. And then it was time to touch him. She was supposed to be calming herself in preparation for the next hour and a half, but her heart wouldn't stop racing.

Faking tranquility, she moved to his side and started her usual routine. "Okay, Cal, are you comfortable? The headrest is adjustable if you need me to move it up or down."

"I'm good."

"Then let's begin. Let me know if the pressure is too heavy or too light, or I've reached a sensitive area."

Brenna rubbed her hands together, warming them. Then she folded the blanket down from his waist, leaving the sheet pulled up to his shoulders. She could do this. She'd done this thousands of times since graduating from massage school almost four years ago.

It was just that she hadn't even wanted to touch a man

with more than purely professional intentions in ages. And now that a guy had finally piqued her interest—a guy who didn't even live in Boston, she reminded herself—her professions' ethical limitations chafed in a way they never had before. Life was so unfair sometimes.

But her hormones had waited this long; they could suck it up and wait a little longer. Forever, if they had to. She wasn't going to do anything to jeopardize the referral relationship she'd painstakingly developed with the Rajah. The dozen or so outcall clients the hotel sent her way every month often made the difference between barely scraping by, and being able to save a little toward next month's expenses.

She rested her hands at the base of Cal's spine, on top of the sheet. Then she began a series of long strokes that smoothed the sheet against him from the top of his glutes up to his shoulders and down again, until he started to relax. Only then did she undrape his upper body, folding the sheet across his firm butt and tucking it in under each hip.

It was like unwrapping a long-anticipated present. Cal's broad, beautifully muscled back greeted her, a few little freckles scattered here and there along his V-shaped torso. His well-defined traps and delts gave way to heavy triceps. She was looking forward to the pure sensuality of smoothing slick fingers and palms across warm skin and taut muscle. At least *that* was well within the bounds of propriety.

She warmed some oil in her palms before placing her hands between his shoulders, at the top of his spine. Pausing, she savored the first moment of skin-to-skin connection. She visualized healing energy passing through her tingling palms into Cal's tense muscles. With her pulse beating heavily in her throat, she began the slow, gliding motions of effleurage, up and down his back.

Then, forcing her attraction to him into abeyance, she started on his shoulders in earnest. A pained sound escaped him as she began to knead the twin knots where his neck met his torso.

"Cal? Is this too much?"

"Ohhhh, God. I can take it. It's okay." Each burst of words came out in a rush, as if she were squeezing them out of him with every press against the bunched-up muscles.

Brenna couldn't tell if he was trying to convince her or himself, so she eased off as she compressed the trigger points that riddled his back and shoulders. She'd had clients as tense as Cal before, but not many of them.

His breath escaped on a pained hiss when she tugged against one of his shoulder blades, working her fingers into the knots hiding underneath. "Do you ever talk with your clients while you're working?" he asked.

"Sure. Need some distracting?"

"Yeah." The word sounded almost like a groan. "Something to take my mind off these knots. I had no idea I had so many."

Sports was always a safe topic. "Have you watched any Red Sox games while you've been in town?"

"Yesterday's game was unbelievable," he said. "Did you see it?"

"I didn't get home until the eighth inning, but I caught Pedroia's two-run homer in the ninth."

"You're a Sox fan?"

"I've lived here for nine years," she said drily. "It's kind of hard not to be to some degree."

"Where are you from originally? You look like you're from an island in the South Pacific or something."

Brenna stiffened, then forced herself to relax. Maybe he didn't mean anything by it. Not everyone was like Gregory's awful family. She would operate under that assumption until Cal showed his true colors, whatever they might be.

"California." Then she steeled herself to answer the question he was really asking, the question she'd been asked more times than she could count. "My dad's Japanese. His family came to the US when he was two. My mom is your quintessential blonde and blue-eyed California girl." As she spoke, her hands continued to press and glide, homing in on areas of tension—which was pretty much all of him. Lord, did this man need bodywork.

"Ah, that's cool," he said. "Do you speak Japanese?"

Her concern faded. "A little. My dad didn't really speak it except with my grandparents. I actually speak more Spanish. Some French, too."

"I wish I spoke another language. I took French in high school, but it didn't stick."

"Quel dommage," she teased him.

"I remember that one! 'What a shame.'"

She imagined his grin—lopsided and adorably sexy. Too bad he was lying on his stomach, so she couldn't see it.

"I'm a Sox fan too, actually," he said after a moment.

"Because they're playing well?"

"No, I'm legit. Grew up in New Hampshire."

"Local boy makes good, eh?" She smiled, even though he couldn't see her.

"Something like that."

The tension ebbed from Cal's upper body as he underwent her ministrations, and they both fell silent. Brenna enjoyed this aspect of her profession the most—helping her clients find peace, both physical and emotional. Cal's breathing began to slow and even out, and her own gradually matched it.

She moved to his lower back, applying deep pressure as she slid her hands a little way underneath the sheet, then around to the back of his hips. He stiffened up again; this area was plagued by trigger points as well.

"Cal? Would you like me to work these knots in your hips and glutes?" The question was part of her standard routine, but on him it felt way more sensual than normal. And not just because the man had a tremendously fine ass.

"Mmm. Yeah. The knots hurt a bit, but it feels so good when you're done with them."

His thick, sleepy voice sent an inappropriate shiver up her spine. *Down, girl!*

She laid one of the towels across his upper back so he wouldn't lose too much heat through his oil-slicked skin. Then she redraped him, exposing his right leg and most of the right side of his chiseled butt.

Warming another generous dollop of oil between her hands, she set to work. One hand rested atop the other, so the weight of her body pressed down through just her right palm.

He let out a groan.

Brenna paused. "Everything okay?"

"Yeah, sorry. I couldn't help it," he murmured, sounding embarrassed.

"No, that's fine. You do what your body needs to do." She circled once again up to his lower back before starting another deep glide across his firm glutes.

After a few minutes, he shifted on the table. She thought nothing of it until she became aware he was tensing in cadence with her massage strokes. His breath, she now noticed, was also hitching almost imperceptibly as her hands rounded the curve of his butt to his hips.

In fact, both his repetitively tensed muscles and his increasingly ragged inhalations were getting more obvious. It was almost like...

Brenna bit her lip. *Oh, shit.* Cal was getting turned on. And a tiny, secret part of her reveled in it.

2

CAL LAY FACEDOWN on the padded table, immensely grateful to his boss for insisting he get a massage. Their client's trial started tomorrow, and Cal had been working his ass off for the past four months getting them ready for it. A lot was riding on the outcome, and not just for their client, Conovan Industries. He was up for partner this year, and a strong performance here could clinch the decision. He needed to be in top form.

Besides, the masseuse was hot, and the massage itself was incredible. Sensual, skirting but never crossing the line to sexual. He had never before been so conscious of his skin as a sensory organ, but now he was hyperaware of every stroke, every press on his back.

The experience was turning out to be surprisingly emotional as well. It had been far too long since anyone had touched him with such complete focus and dedication. Friends-with-benefits and casual relationships—the only kind he'd allowed himself in the past six years—just didn't go there.

He was sort of regretting he hadn't kept his boxer briefs on, though. Especially after he stupidly agreed to let her massage his hips and butt. Lord knew he needed it after being chained to his desk for months on end, but he'd never realized his hips were such an erogenous zone. Until now. He was sporting a hard-on that all the baseball statistics in the world couldn't deflate, and it was both uncomfortable and embarrassing.

Thankfully, she soon covered his back again and shifted her focus farther down. First to one leg, then the other, giving his erection a chance to disappear so he didn't tent the sheet after he turned over.

His reprieve didn't last long, though.

The masseuse raised the sheet and blanket between them to shield her view as he awkwardly rolled over, lowering them only after he settled onto his back. She slid the pillow out from under his calves, then arranged the covers once more.

Cal could hear her removing the doughnut cushion, and he opened his eyes. Immediately, he regretted it. And not just because he almost certainly had unflattering lines on his face. The sexy masseuse was standing behind his head, her attention focused on his body. Her sun-kissed ponytail had drifted across one shoulder while she worked him over. The tip of her pink little tongue poking out from between her lips was the cherry on top.

She leaned forward to fold the covers across his chest. He slammed his eyes shut again, but it was too late.

An image flooded his mind, of dusky nipples close enough for him to lick, of the lightning strike of pleasure that would jolt her if he did. Cal couldn't suppress a slight shudder at the thought.

He swallowed hard. She was only massaging his shoulders and the tops of his pecs, but the desire that lanced through him still went straight to his groin.

The masseuse paused. "Are you cold? I can turn up the heat, if that would help."

Was she serious? "No, thanks. I'm fine," he gritted out. He was hot enough already. More than hot enough. It didn't matter where she touched him now. Every nerve ending in his skin was at full attention and clamoring for more.

He inhaled, filling his lungs as she moved to his right side and started on his arm. Then he exhaled in a slow, even stream, trying to relax. Or at least trying to give her the impression he was relaxed. He concentrated on breathing as evenly as possible while her fingers twined silkily with his, her thumbs rubbing little patterns into his palm.

He did a fair job at maintaining the pretense of disinterest as she switched sides to attend to his other arm and hand. But the facade—and his breathing—grew a little shaky when she began to massage his pecs. Her thumbs grazed his nipples, which immediately tightened into traitorous little nubs. He wondered how much more he'd have to bear before his ninety minutes were up.

When she covered his torso again with the sheet and blanket, he nearly sighed in relief. As frustratingly pleasurable as her touch was, the absence of it for a few moments was a blessing.

Though her next move ratcheted his arousal right back up. She tucked in the covers on either side of his waist, then pressed inward, bracketing his hips with her palms. The small circles she made alternately pulled the blanket taut across his rapidly swelling erection and loosened it again.

Cal stifled a groan, hoping his calm exterior belied his inner turmoil. He didn't even want to strike up a conversation again because he'd just imagine her urging him to let it happen, let her make him feel good—

Okay! Enough! He forced his tense muscles to loosen. That strategy sufficed until she shifted her hands to his upper thigh, working it through the covers, and all he could feel was her fingertips scraping against the edge of his pubic hair through two unwanted layers of material. Just a couple more inches, and she'd be palming his cock.

It was getting more and more difficult to hide how turned on he was. Part of him was desperately hoping he'd make it through the remainder of the massage session without embarrassing himself. The rest of him was unrealistically wishing her hand would slip, or even that she might take pity on him and put him out of his sexual misery.

Finally, she undraped one of his legs and began to tackle yet another set of knots there, and he could stop trying to will away his hard-on. He'd done it. He'd endured, and now he could concentrate on just enjoying whatever was left of the massage. Even though his dick remained unrelentingly rigid, and was probably at this very moment painting glistening trails of pre-come across his belly. At least everything else could finally relax.

Eventually, his poor, neglected cock did, too.

At last, the masseuse rearranged the blanket and covered him up once more, and he realized the session must be coming to an end. She stroked his face with gentle fingertips, from the center of his forehead out to each side. His skin tingled as he soaked up what had to be the last moments of her attentions.

One warm hand cupped his jaw, and a ghostly impression of heat hovered just above his mouth. He knew he had to be hallucinating, yet his lips twitched, trying to pout into a touch, a kiss, that wasn't ever coming.

Before he could force his eyelids open, her hand pulled away from his face. Even though he'd expected it, the shock of the severed connection still reverberated through him like the pure tone of a perfectly-cast bronze bell. Then, as the lingering echo of her fingers and palm against his skin died away, he slowly emerged from the haze of relaxation she'd created.

"Cal," she said, her voice quiet in the stillness, "I'm going to go wash up now. You take your time in here. I'll knock before I come back in."

"Okay." His voice broke across the word. He cleared his throat.

"I'll bring you some water, too." He heard her cross the room. A fan of light spilled out briefly as the bathroom door opened, then closed behind her.

Unable to move, he listened to the water running in the bathroom. He needed to get up and put on some clothes, before she came back. Any minute now, he would do that.

When he couldn't avoid it any longer, he mustered the strength to press his palms against the table, levering himself up as he swung his feet over the side. The masseuse had left a clean towel on the coffee table, so he wrapped it around his waist before stumbling to the closet.

Earlier, he'd laid out a change of clothes on top of his suitcase. He hurried into his underwear and jeans, then shoved his arms through the sleeves of his plaid shirt. He started to button it, but the room was hotter than an August afternoon, so he left his shirt undone and turned up the air-conditioning instead. Then he refolded the towel, placed it back on the coffee table, and sprawled out on the sofa to wait for her.

Several minutes later, she cracked open the door and knocked. "Can I come in?" she called out to him, her voice low and sensual.

"Sure." His own voice was still hoarse, and he was grateful that she was bringing him something to drink.

He sat up straighter as she approached. When she'd first arrived, he'd idly watched her set up the table while his tension headache squeezed his head in a vise. He'd thought she was attractive as she bustled through the task with an economy of movement that spoke to many hours of practice.

Clearly, he hadn't been paying attention. Attractive didn't do her justice. She was stunning.

The exotic tilt at the corners of her golden brown eyes made it hard to look away from her. Her lips were full and kissable. She had a slender frame, with the pert little breasts he'd fantasized about earlier. The gentle curve of her hips flared from a narrow waist.

She handed over the glass, and he thanked her before raising it to his lips. As he swallowed, she said, "You should make sure you drink at least six to eight glasses of water or other clear fluids in the next twenty-four hours."

Cal finished the glass and cleared his throat. "I didn't think it was possible for me to feel this relaxed. That massage was amazing. My headache is totally gone," he said, both pleased and surprised. He gifted her with one of his trial-winning smiles.

"That's great," she said. Then she turned away to start breaking down the table and packing away her supplies into the duffel bag. A faint but unmistakable blush tinted her cheeks, making him regret leaving his chest bare. He just felt so at ease, it hadn't even occurred to him to take her feelings into consideration.

He frowned, annoyed at himself, and stood to belatedly do up his shirt. But it was hard to sustain any negative emotion for long when his bloodstream was rich with massage-induced endorphins. Endorphins convincing him that life was so good right now, nothing could go wrong, which led to his second misstep in as many minutes.

"After you're all packed up, would you like to get some coffee with me downstairs in the lounge? I'd love to get to know you better." Alternatively, or maybe afterward, he'd love to get to know her better right here, in his king-sized bed.

Or maybe not. Her brows had drawn together. Bad sign.

Though he could be reading her wrong. Besides, what did he have to lose? So he tried again, hoping he was correctly guessing the source of her concern. "You can leave your stuff up here if you want, so you don't have to lug it around with you. We can come back and get it whenever you're ready to go."

She straightened to her full height, which still left her well shy of his own six-foot-one. "That's not the issue," she said. "First of all, I don't date my clients. And second of all, if I did date my clients, I certainly wouldn't do it anywhere near the hotel. I have a professional reputation to maintain."

Oh. Duh. His brain must not have come back online yet.

"Right. Well," he soldiered on, as she sped up her packing, "do you have a card? I'll be here for another two weeks or so, maybe we could set up another session—"

She ignored his second attempt altogether. "I, ah, need to get going. Here's the bill for tonight." Looking downright uncomfortable now, she turned to him just long enough to hand him a black leather folio.

Shit. It had been a long time since he'd screwed up this royally with a girl, and her rejection stung. Nevertheless, he scanned the bill and added a very generous tip—courtesy of his boss, who'd offered to pay for the massage in appreciation for Cal's hard work. Then, as she tugged the carrying case's long zipper around the massage table, he shut the folio with an authoritative *thwap*.

She glanced up at him, and he wished he hadn't drawn her attention in that way. But while he had it... "Your name is...Brenna, right?"

She focused again on her gear, zipping her duffel closed. "Yes," she said. Though the word sounded almost like a question.

So he decided to press his luck a little further. "What's your last name?"

Apparently finished with her packing, she straightened. The hesitation in her voice was as unmistakable as the pink that crept back into her cheeks. "It's Nakamura."

"Nice to meet you, Brenna Nakamura." With a smile, he handed her the folio.

"Um, thanks." She bent down to slip it into one of her

duffel's outer pockets, then stood and met his eyes once more. "I'm glad I was able to help you feel better," she said before shouldering the table and duffel.

She waited for him to precede her through the foyer to the door. He was rapidly running out of ways to prolong their encounter. "I know you can manage on your own, but would you like a hand with your things down to the lobby?" he asked as he opened the door.

"No thanks, I'm fine. I do appreciate the offer though." She brushed past him, pausing to look up at him through those dark, thick lashes. "Take care."

"You too."

He watched for a few moments as she walked away, managing the burden of her massage gear with a grace that made it look deceptively easy. Letting out a breath that was almost a sigh, he retreated into his room and allowed the door to close. Might as well get some work done.

But he knew that when he eventually went to bed, he'd be thinking of her.

BRENNA'S PACE QUICKENED once she rounded the corner to the elevator and was sure she was out of Cal's sight. He and those ridged abs of his were just far too tempting. It was a good thing he'd buttoned his shirt before asking her to have coffee with him, or he might have befuddled her into saying yes.

It would definitely be best if she never saw him again. A second massage session would probably end with the undeniable spark between them bursting into flame. She would lose the Rajah Hotel gig—and quite possibly her license and her livelihood—if she showed up at the front desk with her hair a tousled mess and her face glowing with satisfaction.

And it would almost be worth it, too.

Regret dogged her all the way down to the front desk, where it doubled when she pulled out the bill and saw the number Cal had filled in for her tip. Astonished, she handed over the folio to Crystal, the front desk attendant. "He tipped me seventy-five bucks?"

"Looks that way." Crystal smiled. "Guess we have another satisfied guest, Brenna."

"Yeah, but…" All she could do was shake her head as Crystal paid her. The tip was half the bill.

What exactly was Cal trying to express with this gesture? Was he attempting to butter her up? Apologize for the awkward attempt to ask her out? Or was he just grateful that she'd relieved his stress so he could get ready for his upcoming trial?

Now she wished she hadn't ignored his interest in a second session. Purely because of the boost to Serenity Massage's bottom line, of course.

Though she had to admit, it really had been lovely to work on all of those well-defined muscles. Even his infernal rippling abs.

Crystal picked up the phone. "Hang on a sec, let me see if our driver is available."

"That's okay, you don't have to do that." But Crystal waved Brenna's protest away.

The truth was, she was wiped out. When Crystal had called two and a half hours ago, Brenna had been tidying up one of her two tiny but peaceful therapy rooms after her five o'clock client had left, trying not to think about the dire state of her bank account. Three years into her five-year business plan, she was already way off track.

She'd worked in a high-end spa for the better part of a year after finishing her training, and she'd thought that experience had given her a good handle on start-up costs, revenue, and expenses. Serenity Massage was supposed to have been profitable starting almost two years ago, including paying her a salary sufficient to cover the mortgage on her condo and stock her cupboards with more than cereal and dried pasta. Unfortunately, her projections hadn't taken into account an economic down-turn.

To maximize her revenue until the economy picked up again, she now accepted bookings between eight in the morning and nine at night. Though she had a depressingly large amount of downtime, she almost never took a day off.

Brenna's stomach growled, reminding her it was nearly nine o'clock now, and she'd barely had time to grab a bagel and a cup of tea on her way over to the hotel. She'd taken the subway over here, and she was sure her fellow T-riders had been annoyed by how much space her out-call gear took up. But it was late now, and if the hotel's driver was unavailable, her choices were limited—lug her gear ten blocks in the dark, cut into tonight's profits by paying for a taxi, or wait for who knew how long on the subway platform until the next train arrived. The Sunday night public transit schedule didn't offer many options, as she well knew.

Crystal hung up the phone. "Paul's out front. He can take you wherever you need to go."

Brenna's shoulders sagged in relief. "Thanks, Crystal."

She scoffed. "Oh, it was no problem, Brenna. Have a great night."

"Good night."

Brenna found Paul waiting under the glass portico, wearing his monogrammed livery and leaning against the hotel's gleaming black town car. With his usual good cheer, he greeted her in his remarkably thick Boston accent. Then he stowed her gear in the trunk while she got comfortable in the back seat. Her head lolled against the headrest as fatigue descended upon her.

The driver's door closed. "New-bree and Glahsta?" Which—after living in Boston for close to a decade—she automatically translated to "Newbury and Gloucester?"

"Thanks," she said. "That'd be great." The car eased away from the curb.

Paul had been in the business long enough to understand she was too tired to make small talk, for which she was deeply grateful. He delivered her to Serenity Massage's front door less than ten minutes later. When she pulled out her wallet to tip him, he held up a hand. "No need for that, hon'. I can see that you been workin' even hahdah than me."

"You're the best, Paul. If you or your wife ever need a massage, just call me. I'll totally give you a discount."

"Thanks, doll. Lemme get ya things."

After he carefully deposited her gear next to her on the curb, he circled back around to the driver's side and waved. "Have a good one!"

"Same to you," she said as he ducked back inside the limo.

Shouldering her gear one last time, she maneuvered it up the brownstone's exterior stairs. She let herself inside, then schlepped everything up another flight of narrow stairs to the suite.

After storing her gear in the tiny coat closet, she changed back into her street clothes. Her uniform and the soiled sheets and blanket went into the dirty laundry bag, and the hotel's payment and Cal's outlandish tip went into the safe bolted into the utility closet. Only then did she shut off the lights and head home, where she absolutely, positively would not be fantasizing about Cal Wilcox and his perfectly sculpted body.

3

CAL'S ALARM WOKE HIM at quarter-to-five. Well-rested and full of energy—thanks in no small part to Brenna's fantastic massage the night before—he quickly finished revising the witness outline he'd been working on last night. The plaintiff's chief operating officer wouldn't know what hit him once Cal's cross-examination got underway. With an evil grin, he e-mailed the outline to Grant Coburn, the senior partner leading the trial team.

At seven-fifteen, after a workout and a shower, Cal was dressed for court and sipping his orange juice in the cafe downstairs. His toast and Western omelet arrived just as Grant finally showed up.

Grant's bushy eyebrows winged upward as he greeted Cal. He sat down and ordered coffee and a danish. Then he turned back to Cal. "Clearly you took my advice. Good Lord, man. That must have been one hell of a massage!"

Cal's neck heated at the memory of Brenna's hands molding themselves to his hips and butt, but he managed to keep his voice steady. "What makes you say that?"

"You look like the weight of the world dropped off your shoulders."

Cal shrugged, trying to look nonchalant. "It feels that

way, too."

As the two attorneys ate and discussed trial strategy, Cal's mind drifted back to Brenna and the mixed messages she'd been sending last night. She'd seemed extraordinarily uncomfortable with the idea of going out with him, even for a casual cup of coffee. But he hadn't missed the way her eyes had raked his torso when she came back into the room after the massage had ended. She'd been embarrassed that she'd looked, but she'd still done it.

It sank in that Grant was speaking to him. "I'll take a look at the outline over the lunch break. Anything in particular that I should pay attention to?" Grant asked.

Cal snapped his focus back to his boss. "Nah, it's pretty tight at this point. I'm happy with it, and I think the new line of questioning will play well with the jury."

"Good." Grant glanced at his watch. "Time to head over to court. You ready?" He shoved the last bite of his pastry into his mouth and washed it down with the rest of his coffee.

"As I'll ever be." Cal suppressed a smile as he recalled giving Brenna that same answer last night. In reality, he hadn't been prepared at all for the experience, or for the unusual intimacy—both physical and emotional—he'd shared with the beautiful masseuse.

Not that he was looking for an emotional connection right now. After nearly eight years of slavish devotion to Carter, Munroe and Hodges, he was finally up for partner, and he couldn't afford to get sidetracked before the brass ring was within his grasp. Physical connections—so long as they were discreet and infrequent—were fine. Necessary, even. He was a man, after all.

But he'd decided a few years ago that serious relation-ships were off-limits until the partnership question was settled—favorably, he hoped. Afterward, he could spare some time to woo a suitable other half. Someone well-educated, elegant, and classy, whom he could escort with pride and confidence to the Partner Prom, a retreat CMH hosted every year for all the US-based partners and their spouses. Someone who was behind him the way his mom had always supported his dad, who'd been the managing partner of a respected regional law firm in Cal's home-town.

Then again, right now he didn't exactly have time for physical connections, either. It was probably for the best that Brenna had blown him off last night. Cal needed to kick ass at this trial, which meant sixteen- to twenty-hour days until it was over and he headed back to DC.

At least the case against their client was weak. The plaintiff was claiming Conovan had hired one of its em-ployees in violation of a non-compete agreement and had stolen its trade secrets. But Cal had been involved with this case since the very beginning, and he knew Conovan's defense was supported by strong evidence, and their wit-nesses were well-prepared and credible. It had taken a lot of travel to Conovan's offices in the Boston suburbs to get them that way, though.

After so much time on the road, he was seriously considering moving his practice up to Boston. Conovan wasn't his only client in southern New England. Although CMH had a corporate practice in Boston already, rumor had it the partnership was considering expanding the office to a full-service operation. Cal wasn't going to do anything to screw up his chances of making partner, but if all went well and they elected him to the partnership at the end of the summer, maybe a transfer would be in order.

They were approaching the courthouse steps now, and he realized he and Grant hadn't exchanged a word during the entire walk. Grant must have been mentally preparing to deliver the opening statement on behalf of their client. While Cal, on the other hand, had been day-dreaming. Time to get his head back in the game.

Soon they were seating themselves at the defense counsel's table in one of the smaller courtrooms in the historic Suffolk County courthouse. Renee, their paralegal, told him their audiovisual equipment was set up and ready to go. The jury filed in, and Cal's pulse rate accelerated as the bailiff brought the courtroom to order and announced Judge Maureen Cooke.

After Judge Cooke sat down and the bailiff swore in the jury, she said a few introductory words. Then she invited the plaintiff's counsel to begin her opening statement, and it was game on.

Plaintiff's counsel stood up. She wore a conservative navy-blue skirt suit, and her dark brown hair was pinned back. Taking a position about ten feet from the jury, she introduced herself and her client. Then she began describing the evidence the jury would see and the reasons why the defendant should be found liable.

Cal scanned the jurors as they listened to her presentation. Many seemed attentive, though a few appeared bored, staring out the window rather than watching her.

Fifteen minutes later, Grant took her place. He faced

the jury in his impeccably tailored charcoal-gray suit, starched white dress shirt, and dark blue tie with a coordinating sky blue paisley pocket square. His opening statement was much livelier in comparison, in keeping with both Grant's personal style and CMH's apparently greater resources. Unlike the plaintiff's presentation, Grant's speech was interspersed with video clips and blowups of key pieces of evidence. Cal observed jurors nodding in agreement at several points during Grant's opening, and they seemed to be paying closer attention.

Grant finished and sat down, and the plaintiff called its first witness—the CEO of the company. As the direct examination progressed, Cal typed furiously on his laptop. He wasn't surprised that the CEO was testifying about substance and not just fluff. In fact, he was glad. This opened the door to many more lines of cross-examination than they might otherwise have been allowed to pursue.

Cal suppressed a smile. This trial was going to be fun.

BUT AFTER TWO FULL WEEKS of it—accompanied by late nights, last-minute additions to witness lists, and rulings that each side thought favored the other—tempers on both sides of the courtroom were wearing thin.

Opposing counsel had made so many groundless objections during Grant's and Cal's witness examinations that a few of the jurors had begun rolling their eyes whenever she opened her mouth. So Cal took inordinate pleasure in his opponent's scowl when Judge Cooke ended the day ten minutes early, rather than allowing her to start her cross-examination right before they broke for the weekend. Just as Grant had planned it.

Sucks to be you, counselor, Cal thought. But he forced his expression to remain neutral as everyone stood and waited for Her Honor to exit the courtroom.

As the last jurors left, Cal and Renee began collecting their papers and shutting down their laptops. Grant suggested that they drop off their stuff at the hotel, then meet in the lobby at six-thirty and walk over to this fantastic nouveau French restaurant on Newbury Street for dinner before calling it a night. And "fantastic," to Grant, likely meant an unparalleled gastronomic experience, complete with hundred-dollar bottles of wine and maybe even a nice single-malt scotch or artisanal bourbon afterward.

Cal stuffed his laptop and cord into his bag. "Sounds perfect."

"Yep, count me in." Renee's straight brown hair bobbed around her face as she nodded.

The three parted ways at the nearest cab stand. Grant and Renee caught a taxi back to the hotel, but Cal decided to take advantage of the glorious late-spring afternoon and walk over from the courthouse. Maybe fifteen minutes of exercise and a glimpse of the Public Garden would reenergize him.

As he had hoped, the walk provided a welcome change from the tense atmosphere in the courtroom. Though he perked up even more when he got to the hotel's lower lobby. A few steps ahead of him was a familiar dark-brown ponytail, swishing in time with the measured steps of his favorite masseuse. Once again, she was hauling that duffel and massage table, which still seemed like they ought to be far too heavy for her slender frame.

"Brenna?" he called out before he could think better of it. He'd have to wing this. Although he preferred not to leave important things to chance, sometimes opportunities had to be seized when they arose. It was as true in the courtroom as in the bedroom.

She turned to look behind her, her bags swaying with the movement. Recognition widened her eyes as he closed the gap between them.

Now he was near enough for the scent of her massage oil to drift into his nostrils. His body hardened, remembering her silky touch.

"Cal?" Her attention darted down to his chest, then up to his face again.

He realized he must look very different from the last time she'd seen him—when he'd been bare-chested and acting like an ass. There'd be none of that, this time. Trial attorneys were confident, every move planned out ahead, yet ready to roll with the punches when things took an unusual direction. Besides, it wasn't like he hadn't been hoping for a chance encounter with her, just like this one.

He straightened, dragging his fingers through his hair, and gave her his most appealing and genuine smile. "Hey. I'm glad I ran into you like this. How've you been?"

"Fairly busy. But that means business is good, so I can't complain." She offered him a friendly smile; all was apparently forgiven and forgotten. "How about you? How's your trial going?"

"Great. We should be finished early next week."

"Well, I hope you win." She glanced down the hall toward the elevator. "I'm afraid I need to get going, though."

Only then did it sink in that she must be on her way to see another client at the hotel. An irrational surge of envy had him fighting the urge to clench his hands into fists. He couldn't even ask her to dinner tonight because he already had plans with Grant and Renee—plans he'd been looking forward to until about a minute ago.

He could carve out some time this weekend, though. A late night would be worth it, if it meant spending another couple of hours getting to know Brenna. He needed to eat anyway; why not with her? The worst that could happen was she'd say no. As his dad had always said, if you don't ask, you don't get.

He rested two fingertips against the smooth skin at the back of Brenna's hand. Keeping his voice low, he asked, "Have dinner with me tomorrow night? If you're free, that is."

She had started to turn away from him, but pivoted back at his question. The warmth in her eyes had him wanting to reach out and brush back a few strands of hair that had come loose from her ponytail.

"Ummm…" Her gaze slid sideways. Crap—she was going to shoot him down again.

"Wait. Before you say no, it wouldn't be a date."

Her forehead crinkling, she considered the statement he was already wishing he could retract. "What do you mean, not a date?"

"You said last time you don't date your clients. So this wouldn't be a date. You do eat dinner, right?"

She nodded, still reluctant.

"We'll just be two hungry people, sharing a meal." He was watching her closely as he said these words, and he smiled when the tension in her shoulders eased. She was going to say yes. "Since I don't know the area, you pick the place. And time," he added. "I'm flexible."

She exhaled a long breath. "Okay. But I'm booked tomorrow night."

Sunday would be more difficult since he needed to be in court the next morning, but he would take what he could get. "How about Sunday?"

Her shoulders dropped as she let out another nervous exhalation. Then she nodded decisively. "Yeah. Sunday should work." She paused. "Do you prefer Indian or pizza?"

His smile broadened. "Pizza sounds great."

"There's a place about three blocks down Newbury Street from here, Ciro's. It has the best Neapolitan-style pizza in Boston."

"Sold."

She looked up at him. "Would eight-thirty be too late?"

"Nope. Perfect." He paused. "Should I pick you up somewhere, or meet you there...?"

"Um, we can meet there." She fumbled in her duffel before pulling a business card from one of the outer pockets. "Here's my card, with my cell phone. You know, in case you can't find the place, or need to change plans."

He glanced down at the card, then back up at her. Her flushed cheeks were frickin' adorable.

Not to be outdone, Cal extracted a black leather card case from the breast pocket of his suit jacket and plucked out a cream-colored card on heavyweight stock. CMH didn't stint. "My cell and e-mail are on there, if you need them." Their eyes met. "But I'm sure we'll be just fine."

She took his card, but tension crept into her shoulders once more. "I really do need to go now. I'm going to be late."

He nodded toward her duffel. "Can I carry one of those bags for you, at least up to the lobby? I'm headed that way myself."

She actually looked tempted this time, but still refused his offer. "I'm okay. It's easier for me to have them both. It helps balance the load."

"If you're sure."

He remained at her side as they rode the elevator up to the main lobby, the melodic lilt of her voice keeping him entirely focused on her as they talked about the unseasonably hot May weather and the little herb garden she was growing on her roof deck.

"There are a lot of things I'm good at," he said. "Keeping green things alive unfortunately isn't one of them."

Her golden brown eyes lit up. "I know a plant I bet even you couldn't kill."

He arched an eyebrow dubiously.

"I'm serious," she protested.

He'd been enjoying their banter, but when the elevator door opened, rendering them visible from the front desk, her demeanor became noticeably more distant.

"It was good seeing you, Cal," she said as she stepped out. As if this encounter was going to be the last time she laid eyes on him.

A reminder was in order. "I'm looking forward to Sunday night."

She regarded him for a long moment. Then she

nodded once. "Yes. Of course."

He watched her walk away, her hips gently swaying. If he stayed much longer, she would catch him at it when she stopped at the front desk. So he circled around to the main elevator bank and entered Brenna's contact information into his phone before heading up to his room to get ready for dinner.

A scant hour later, Cal was perusing the menu at L'Avenue, hard-pressed to choose between the smoked oysters with truffled potato cakes appetizer and the hearty bouillabaisse. At least he already knew what he was going to order for his entrée—the medallions of veal in tomato and shallot sauce, which came with tender baby green beans sautéed with garlic and pine nuts. In the meantime, he was stuffing himself liberally with the steaming bread rolls that had been placed on their table by their most attentive server, and was relaxing with a glass of pinot noir that Grant, a wine connoisseur, had picked out.

"Cal, I'd wanted to discuss a change in strategy with you," Grant said.

"Sure, what's up?"

"I think you should do the closing."

"Me? Really?" A grin spread across Cal's face. Though his exultation was quickly tempered when he contemplated how late he would need to work this weekend if he still wanted to spend a few hours with Brenna. He wasn't going to cancel on her unless the situation on Sunday night was dire.

"While you were putting those witnesses through their paces these past two weeks—which was a thing of beauty, by the way—I was watching the jury. You really seemed to be connecting well with them. All we need is ten out of the twelve to go our way, and I think you're the one to make it happen."

Grant's confidence warmed Cal's chest with pride. "Thanks for giving me this opportunity. I won't let CMH or Conovan down." Or himself, for that matter. This was a golden opportunity to cinch the partnership. Assuming, of course, he didn't screw it up.

"I know that, Cal. I wouldn't trust you with the closing argument if I didn't believe you could bring it home for us."

Their appetizers arrived, and they all dug in. After taking a couple of bites in a bliss-induced silence, Grant said, "So, tomorrow you should take a look at the slide deck and the outline for the closing. Tweak them however you like, and I'll review what you've put together tomorrow night. Then I want you to run through it with me or Renee a couple of times on Sunday. You already know what a big difference that makes."

"Of course I do. I'll dive in as soon as we get back to the hotel," Cal assured him.

The rest of their meal, which was as exquisite as Cal had expected, was much less eventful. After finishing their coffee and after-dinner drinks, the trio enjoyed a leisurely walk back to the hotel in the balmy evening air. They parted ways in the elevator with plans to meet up the next morning for breakfast in the café before heading over to CMH's offices and yet another long day of trial prep.

As Cal unlocked the door to his room, a jolt of adrenaline quick-started his heart. He'd be seeing Brenna again in forty-eight hours, and he had a closing argument to whip into shape in the meantime. Not to mention some judicious strategizing about how he might be able to convince a certain skittish masseuse to go to bed with him after dinner Sunday night. But blowing away the jury—and Grant—next week took precedence over everything else.

Good thing multitasking was one of Cal's specialties.

4

AFTER UNEXPECTEDLY RUNNING into Cal at the Rajah late that afternoon, Brenna had floated through the rest of her day. Luckily her clients hadn't noticed she'd been on autopilot.

For the past two weeks, she'd been trying unsuccessfully to put thoughts of the sexy attorney out of her head. Then he'd called her name in that husky baritone straight from her fantasies. She almost hadn't recognized him in a slate-gray pinstriped suit and a snowy-white dress shirt, collar unbuttoned.

She'd thought bare-chested, casual Cal was hot—who wouldn't?—but the commanding, confident man she'd met this afternoon looked like he could handle anything that came his way. Even her. It hadn't taken much to convince her to go to dinner with him.

Now she was enjoying the unusually warm Friday night on her Charlestown roof deck with a few friends. She supplied the venue, they supplied the refreshments.

Seated across the weathered teak patio table from her was Cissy—Clarissa—who'd worked with her at McKinsey. Cissy's coppery curls, laughing green eyes, and freckles had stood out like a beacon of friendliness in the room full of soberly dressed, newly minted management consultants. Each had quickly become the other's biggest supporter and closest confidante.

Cissy was also the only thing Brenna missed after she'd left McKinsey—well, that and the regular paycheck. The two of them had managed to remain close in the nearly five years since then.

Completing the foursome around Brenna's table were Melanie and Erika, who'd been renting the apartment below her condo for the past few years. Those two cracked her up on a regular basis, complaining about the latest insanity at their jobs or providing color commentary on the men they were dating or sleeping with. Mel's pixie-cut jet-black hair suited her elfin features, pale skin, and wide blue-gray eyes. Rikki was a brash, brassy blonde with curves that Brenna fought not to envy.

At the moment, Rikki and Mel were trying to sell Cissy and Brenna on a movie they wanted to see tomorrow night. While a "rom com with eye candy" sounded appealing, Brenna demurred.

"Aww," Mel said, a sympathetic expression on her face. "Do you have to work again?"

"Yeah. But that's a good thing, even though I wish I could go with you guys."

Rikki looked at Mel. Shrugging, Rikki raised an eyebrow. "We could go on Sunday night."

"Umm...actually..." Brenna's face heated. "I'm not free Sunday night, either." She hadn't intended to tell her friends about Cal, but she felt herself grinning like a fool at the prospect of seeing him again.

The silence stretched until Rikki broke it. "Come on. You can't leave us hanging, with your face all glowing like that."

"Okay," Brenna said, "if you must know. I met someone interesting a couple of weeks ago, and we're going to have dinner Sunday night."

She should have known they wouldn't accept her vague explanation without pressing for details. After all, two pitiful dates in the three years since she'd hung out Serenity Massage's shingle was an embarrassingly poor track record. It almost made her wish she could go back to the fancy day spa gig she'd landed after finishing massage school. At least she'd had some semblance of a life back then, even if she *had* ended up with all the worst shifts.

"You met someone? When did you have a chance to meet someone?" Cissy asked.

Mel piped up. "Yeah, the only guys you meet are—"

"Oh, shit. Don't tell me he's a client." Now Cissy was frowning.

"Well… It's a bit complicated," Brenna admitted before drinking a big slug of her wine.

Her friends stared at her, dumbfounded. "Brenna, you didn't!" Rikki finally managed to splutter.

"Not exactly," Brenna sighed. She took another large sip of wine that closely resembled a gulp.

Rikki was growing exasperated at the pace of her reluctant confession. "Look, before we resort to waterboarding you, just spill it, okay?"

Maybe the impending ordeal would be a little more bearable with a little less sobriety. After draining half her glass, Brenna gathered her courage and tried to describe her feelings about gorgeous, confident Cal.

Once she got started, the words just came tumbling out. She told them about his athlete's body. His captivating silvery-gray gaze. His sexy, rumpled blond hair. Not to mention those abs she still hadn't been able to stop thinking about, dammit.

She had some misgivings about going to dinner with him, though. And not just because he'd been a client of hers a bit too recently for comfort. The chemistry was definitely there, but then again, she'd felt that way about Gregory during college, and look where that had landed her.

"That smug asshole really did a number on you." Cissy's green eyes blazed in solidarity. "You have nothing to be ashamed of. You're a fabulous massage therapist, you're smart, and you're beautiful. And Gregory is an idiot."

"And a pencil-dick," Rikki chimed in, even though she'd never had the misfortune of meeting Brenna's ex-boyfriend.

The tension broken, they all dissolved in giggles.

When their mirth subsided, Cissy said, "Cal must be pretty special if he persuaded you to go out with him. No matter what, I'm proud of you."

"Well," Brenna confessed, "he kind of persuaded me by saying it wouldn't be a date."

Rikki made a disparaging noise. "Give me a break. That's the oldest trick in the book."

Mel shook her head, smiling in apparent agreement.

Concerned, Brenna digested Rikki's opinion. "You guys know I don't date clients." *Not even the hot ones.* She looked around the table. "Do you think I should cancel?"

"I have no idea whether he meant it or not," Cissy said. She shot a glare at Rikki and Mel. "And neither do you two. This is Brenna's first date—or whatever—in, like, more than two years. Let's be supportive, all right?"

But it was too late. Brenna's elation had fizzled. "I don't want to talk about it anymore," she said. "New subject!"

Cissy gave her a long, searching look before asking about everyone's plans for the Memorial Day weekend. Brenna had been too poor to vacation anywhere worth bragging about since her McKinsey days—when she hadn't had time to take vacations. She was nevertheless grateful her best friend had moved the conversation's focus off Brenna's pathetic love life.

She fetched another bottle of wine and some nibblies as their conversation continued. The girls polished off the second bottle over the course of the next hour, with Mel and Rikki calling it a night not too long after that.

Cissy lingered in Brenna's foyer after the others had left. "Can I ask you a question, Bren?"

"Sure." Brenna plucked at the hem of her T-shirt.

"I know you don't date clients, but if you never gave Cal another massage—professionally, I mean—when would he stop being a client?"

Brenna had never tried to come up with a timeline for that question before. She'd never had reason to. Not getting involved with clients had always just been the rule, in black and white, drummed into her at massage school during more than a year of coursework. It was a rule that made sense, to ensure her clients respected her professional boundaries. Besides, she'd never had any inclination to break it until now.

But Cal wasn't likely to become a regular of hers, not with him living in DC. So where did that leave them?

"Uh... That is an excellent question, Ciss. I don't know." Then she grinned. "Yesterday?"

Cissy smiled. "Just some food for thought. I know you don't know him very well, but it's been an insanely long time since I've heard you talk about a man the way you were talking about him."

"Thanks, Ciss." Brenna could always count on her to see right to the heart of a matter.

"Of course. Anyway, I'd better go. Ash is getting off shift soon." A genuinely happy smile lit Cissy's face. Her boyfriend worked in McKinsey's IT department, but she was on the road so often they saw a lot less of each other than in a typical workplace romance.

"How are things going with him? I didn't get to ask you earlier."

"Great. Really great." Cissy opened the door to the condo, apparently not planning to divulge any details before she left.

"Hey. Is that all you're going to say about it?"

"Call me after your not-date." One of Cissy's reddish-brown brows lifted. "We can fill each other in."

"I was already planning to," Brenna said mock-huffily, and Cissy laughed.

"So good to see you, Bren." Cissy hugged her.

"You too, Ciss. Good night."

Cissy waved, then headed downstairs. Brenna pushed the door shut and shot the deadbolt home.

Normally, two glasses of wine at the end of a long week sent her straight off to bed. But tonight, she decided she would indulge in a bath first. Her shoulders and hands were tired, and it was way too late to see if the therapist she sometimes swapped massages with—the one she'd started seeing when the stress of her management consulting job had risen to unbearable levels, actually—had a free half hour.

I bet Cal would do it. She ignored the insidiously appealing thought and turned on the taps to start the tub filling while she washed her face and brushed her teeth. *I bet he'd be good at it too, with those big, strong hands.*

The soaking tub was only a third full, but she stripped off her clothes and slid into its welcoming heat anyway, desperate to relax. Today had been long, and her first booking tomorrow was at eight-thirty, with her last appointment ending more than twelve hours later. Sunday was going to be only slightly less hectic, though at least dinner with Cal would be her reward.

Brenna was thrilled business was so good at the moment. Hopefully it signaled the economy's emergence from the recession. Just in the nick of time.

Every month, she circled three dates on her calendar in red—the due dates for her small business loan payment, her sky-high rent for Serenity Massage's tiny suite on Newbury Street, and the mortgage payment on her condo. And every month when one of these days approached, her stomach roiled as the financial cushion she'd built up at McKinsey evaporated a little more.

Her long workdays weren't enough to get her out of the woods yet by any stretch of the imagination, but at least this month ought to be profitable. The thing was, days like the ones she'd had lately took a lot out of her. She'd be dead on her feet by her nonexistent lunch break tomorrow if she didn't shut her mind up and get to sleep soon.

Cal could help you with that tooooo, her evil little inner voice singsonged.

Brenna's inner voice was undoubtedly correct.

Cal had gotten hard during his massage session— twice, not that she'd been counting or anything—and to her surprise, it had been unbelievably erotic. Not sleazy, not disgusting, not any of the uniformly negative descriptions other massage therapists had supplied when they'd shared war stories with her. Because as turned on as he'd been, he hadn't stepped even the least bit out of line. In fact, his control over his body had been masterful. He hadn't been able to completely control his physiological response, but his breathing had mostly stayed slow and calm, and his muscles had been relaxed enough to fool someone who wasn't trained to read the tiniest nuances of a client's reaction to her touch.

She wanted that oh-so-controlled man to come undone. With her.

Leaning back against the side of the tub, she shivered, considering the idea. Meanwhile, the deliciously steaming water crept past her hips, tickling her abdomen before gradually buoying her breasts.

She couldn't quite bring herself to imagine them in his room, on the feather-soft white cotton duvet covering the enormous bed. The hotel staff might find out somehow. Nor back at Serenity Massage, bent over one of her massage tables. Just…way too tawdry. She would never be able to work in there again without embarrassment.

With the water almost up to the tub's overflow valve, she shut off the faucet. Tiny air bubbles clung to her skin. The barest touch was enough to brush them off, and she watched as they floated to the surface before disappearing. Then she deliberately skimmed her right hand down, past her belly. Her fingertips grazed through the dark thatch of her pubic hair, setting free another cloud of bubbles.

Yes, she'd have him here, in her condo. In her Mission-style dark oak bed, covered with her sensuous raw silk bedspread. Where she could glance over at the wall mirror reflecting the two of them, that toned ass of his flexing rhythmically as she dug her fingers into it, grinding herself against him with each stroke.

She imagined Cal's fingertip resting on her clit for a pulse beat or two before beginning an easy circling motion. Since it was a fantasy, the exquisite rasp of his tongue would soon replace his finger, which would take the opportunity to slip inside her wetness.

Squirming, she enjoyed the sensation of the fleshy ball of her palm against her engorged nub, a fingertip dipping into her entrance. She was so slick with wanting him that nothing would stop his cock from sliding straight home in an ineffable moment of pure pleasure.

She brought herself up slowly, the tension coiling in her muscles as she drew nearer and nearer to the climax she sought. Cal would fuck her like that. Relentless in his onslaught before backing off to tease her with hot kisses and nips, driving her ever higher as she spiraled upward.

More. She needed more. With her free hand, Brenna pinched and rolled first one nipple, then the other. She exulted in the lightning shocks of pleasure shooting through her body.

Her other hand impatiently picked up the pace. Slow and steady wasn't cutting it anymore. Now she needed hard, and fast, and rough. A man as tightly wound as Cal would definitely need that too.

Increasing the pressure on her clit, she rubbed it in urgent little circles, then just back and forth as she got closer. Now two fingertips delved into her, not nearly thick enough or deep enough, but hinting at the penetration she desired. Almost there...

He would fill her perfectly, their pleasure as intertwined as their bodies when they hit their peak. She imagined his sexy groan as his thick shaft spurted into her, his eyelids shuttered and his head thrown back. Her own orgasm washed over her then in an intense, rolling wave that left her gasping.

Slowly, the little contractions and twitches ebbed away into the soothing heat of the tub. She slumped back, resting her head against the tub's edge as her heart rate slowed. Being enveloped in warm water came in a distant second place to actual postcoital cuddling, but it had been so long since she'd experienced the latter, the thought seemed almost as dreamlike as her fantasy.

Beads of sweat trickled down from her temples as blissful relaxation descended upon her. She could barely haul herself out of the water and dry off for bed.

As she lay there alone in the dark, she realized she had two days to forget her fantasy had ever happened. Or she'd be fighting the temptation Sunday night to find out whether Cal was as good a lover in real life as he'd been in her daydreams.

5

BRENNA ARRIVED AT CIRO'S on Sunday a few minutes early, anxiously scanning the entryway for Cal. The restaurant was pleasant and welcoming, but nothing fancy. Sturdy wooden chairs butted up against glass-topped tables, a tea light and bud vase on each one. Frosted globes dangled above the dining area, casting a glow she'd always thought was kind of romantic. Until tonight, when she'd looked at it from the perspective of her not-date with Cal.

She was suddenly and painfully aware of the difference in their financial situations—she a struggling small business owner, he by all indications a successful, up-and-coming attorney. How might the restaurant appear to him? Shabby? Cheap? Lowbrow? Brenna had always cared more about the quality of the food being served than a restaurant's ambiance, but not everyone felt that way.

Cringing inside, she recalled a particularly unpleasant brunch with Gregory and his parents, not too long before he'd broken up with her. His parents had complained nonstop about the adorable diner she'd selected for its delicious comfort food and friendly service. It had been clear from their frowns and pursed lips that they'd thought her choice reflected poorly on her. And that someone like her wasn't good enough for their son, and never would be.

Brenna consciously pushed aside her negative thoughts. At least she knew she'd have a delicious meal tonight, no matter how the not-date turned out.

"Hey."

Cal's greeting startled her out of her musings. She looked up, drawn unerringly to his warm and direct gaze.

"Hi," she said, just as breathless as if two days hadn't passed since she'd last seen him. He was devastatingly sexy in a brown leather jacket over a light blue polo shirt, with flat-front jeans that hung just right on his muscled frame. Brenna was also wearing jeans, along with a teal green scoop-necked sweater and black ballet flats. She always felt a vague sense of relief when she shed her uniform at the end of each workday, but today she'd been excited to change back into the street clothes she'd chosen with Cal in mind.

"This place smells incredible!" he said. "Thanks for suggesting it. I never would've known about it otherwise." He was looking around the restaurant with an open and eager expression, and Brenna relaxed.

"I made a reservation. Sometimes there can be a wait, and I'm starving." She smiled at him nervously before stepping up to the podium to give her name to the hostess.

"Well, we can't have that." His husky rumble made her imagination skip straight over dinner to the part where she invited him back to her condo and took him up on the unspoken promise lurking beneath his words.

"Two hungry people sharing a meal," she muttered in a futile attempt to rein in her hormones.

"What?"

"Nothing," she said airily. "Let's eat."

The hostess seated them at a small table off to the side. The setting wasn't private by any means, but it was quieter than the main dining room, for which Brenna was grateful. She'd never realized how noisy Ciro's was before, when she was eating there by herself or with a friend. On a not-date, however, she didn't want to have to shout to be heard.

Cal steered the conversation to noncontroversial topics as they waited for their server, put in their orders, and settled down to wait for their meals. After a few minutes, the server returned with the red wine Cal had selected and a basket of focaccia.

Brenna watched, amused, as the bottle was formally presented to Cal for inspection. He winked at her when the server bent to pour a taste for his approval. After filling each of their glasses, the server left them to enjoy their wine.

"That whole tasting thing is such a sham." She took a sip of perfectly acceptable cabernet. "It's not like anyone ever sends it back, unless they're trying to get free wine or something."

"I dunno. One time I was at this insanely expensive restaurant with a couple of partners after we'd finished taking a deposition in Atlanta." He idly swirled the dark ruby liquid in his glass. "They were both totally into wine, and the guy who tasted it said it was fine. But when the other guy tried it, he insisted that this three-hundred-dollar bottle they'd just opened and poured for us hadn't been aged properly and had sour notes, so he sent it back." Cal shook his head mournfully. "I tried it before they took it away, and it was still better than any wine I'd ever had before. Or since. I have no idea what he was talking about."

She raised her glass. "To untutored palates."

"I'll drink to that."

Candlelight glinted along the rim of Cal's glass as it clinked against hers, and was reflected as glowing pinpoints in his silvery eyes.

Brenna glanced away. *Not a date.* Though she was starting to wish it was. At this point, she was getting used to the idea Cal was no longer a client, so long as they never had another professional massage session. Easily managed, since he'd be going back to DC after his trial ended—a thought that was far more disappointing than it ought to have been.

Masking her emotions, she plucked a piece of still-warm bread out of the basket. "You should try the focaccia. They bake it here."

"Okay." He selected a piece, too. "So, how did a masseuse from California end up in Boston?"

She suppressed a wince. Correcting his terminology might embarrass him, but it was still going to be the easiest part of her answer. "Massage therapist, if you don't mind."

He paused, bread halfway to his mouth. "Oh! Sorry about that."

"No problem." Now she just had to explain her cross-country relocation without revealing too much. She took a sip of wine to moisten her dry throat.

How much of the story should she divulge? Gregory had moved back to Boston after graduation to work in his family's real estate management business, and he'd asked her to come with him. They'd lived in one of his family's apartments—a gorgeous brownstone they never could have afforded on their own, even with their generous salaries. And then he'd unceremoniously ejected her from his life, because she no longer fit into it.

There was no way in hell she wanted to get too far into that when she and Cal were just starting to get to know each other. So she leaned toward him, as if they were about to share a juicy piece of gossip, and lowered her voice conspiratorially. "Well, you see, there was this guy…" She trailed off, not needing to tell him the ending to that familiar story. "But you probably don't want to hear about that." She looked up at him earnestly from under her lashes and changed the subject. "Besides, I want to hear more about you, Cal."

"How about the nutshell version?" he offered.

She nodded, grateful to have dodged that particular conversational bullet.

"I grew up in Portsmouth, New Hampshire. Went to Brown undergrad and then straight through to law school at Stanford."

The perfect moment dangled right there, when she should tell him she'd gone to college at Stanford, too. They could try to figure out whether their time at her alma mater had overlapped, and whether they knew anyone in common.

But then he would ask how a Stanford grad had ended up as a massage therapist instead of working at a high-tech start-up, or as a lawyer or investment banker or some other so-called respectable profession. After Gregory, she just couldn't bring herself to let an obviously successful guy like Cal judge her that way. And find her lacking.

Besides, it wasn't like this farce of a date would ever go anywhere.

So, with a pang of guilt for not trusting him, she seized on a different commonality to keep their conversation flowing. "I grew up about forty-five minutes from there, in Santa Cruz. Did you like the Bay Area?"

"I loved it out there. Wish I could have stayed."

"Why didn't you?"

He leaned toward her, and she mirrored him, eagerly anticipating his response. Then he said conspiratorially, "Well, you see, there was this girl…"

She laughed, and he joined in. "Okay, I walked into that one," she said. "And so the girl enticed you out to DC? Or was there a stop somewhere in between?"

"Yeah, DC. I joined Carter, Munroe and Hodges right out of law school. Worked my butt off for the past eight years, but I love it, and it seems to be a good fit for me."

Their meals came then, and it was all she could do not to voraciously attack her pizza as soon as it was placed in front of her. As usual, she hadn't had time for lunch, and the energy bar she'd wolfed down between her afternoon clients had long since worn off.

Luckily Cal seemed just as hungry, quickly polishing off his first slice of asparagus and ham before stealing a slice of her porcini and homemade sausage. She raised an eyebrow, but didn't otherwise protest his presumptuousness.

"Pizza tax." He grinned at her before biting off a mouthful of her meal. Then he groaned, his eyes rolling back into his head. After he swallowed, his eyes slowly opened. "Oh my God. That sausage is incredible. I think I'm dying!"

Brenna stilled, her unvoiced protest forgotten as she feasted on his expression. If Cal looked anything like that when he came, it would be the sexiest thing she'd ever see.

She trembled with an unholy eagerness to find out, squeezing her thighs together under the table. This wasn't just a meal between friends. It was foreplay, and it was killing her. Because despite her incredibly hot, incredibly detailed fantasies of bringing Cal back to her place after dinner, she knew it wasn't going to happen. She wasn't a one-night-stand kind of girl. She wasn't even a casual sex kind of girl.

So, with the sparks Cal had set off already incinerating her from within, Brenna played out the charade he'd arranged so she could feel comfortable about going out with him. She swiped a slice of his pizza and bit into it, her eyes never leaving his. Then she swallowed, grinning evilly. Like a friend might do. A non-lustful, non-sex-starved friend who wasn't in the midst of a very lengthy dry spell. "Now we're even."

He shook his head slowly. "Nope." The heat flaring in his eyes was unmistakable. "We're just getting started."

WHAT THE HELL HAD HE been thinking?

As Cal waited for their check, and for Brenna's return from the ladies' room, he believed he knew the answer to that. His brain had taken a back seat to instincts urging him to break from The Plan, for once.

He'd devised The Plan in high school, soon after he'd

decided he wanted to be a partner in a law firm when he grew up—just like his dad. The Plan had evolved over time, but had always channeled his drive and ambition and given him the focus to succeed.

It was why he'd been captain of the high school football team *and* valedictorian. It was why he'd been an Eagle Scout, and why he'd graduated summa cum laude from Brown. It was why he'd been invited to join the Order of the Coif when he'd graduated from law school. And it was why he was now on the verge of beating the odds facing all associates at large law firms, to make partner at one of the most prestigious "BigLaw" firms in the country.

The only problem was, he was six fucking years too late.

Cal had pushed forward with The Plan anyway. It had taken his mind off his grief. But he was having a hard time focusing on achieving his dreams at the moment. For God's sake, in a day or two he'd be delivering the closing argument that could clinch the partnership decision, *if* he performed well. Yet here he was, going out for pizza with a smart, sexy masseuse—massage therapist. And enjoying himself more than any date he'd been on in longer than he cared to admit.

The check finally arrived, bringing him back to reality. Cal looked it over, then stuck his corporate card in the vinyl folder's little pocket.

A few minutes later, Brenna came back to the table and sat down. Her forehead wrinkled into an adorable frown of dismay when she realized that he intended to pay for their meal. "Wait, what are you doing? We should split the bill," she protested.

"Look, I'm just going to expense it anyway. So it's not even like it's me taking you to dinner. It's on the firm."

Her lips flattened. "Fine," she said, though her tone contradicted the sentiment. Then her brows rose into twin arches. "You didn't expense the massage, too, did you? With that enormous tip? I don't want you to get in trouble."

"It's not a problem. My boss paid for that. As a thank-you for my work on the case." His neck heated as he considered how pompous that must sound to her.

But she simply said, "Ah," as if one of the world's great mysteries had been solved.

Even though he knew he shouldn't pry, something compelled him to ask anyway. "Ah, what?"

"Oh." She met his gaze. "Um, I was just thinking that would explain the size of the tip you gave me. Which I was going to thank you for, by the way, but now I guess I should be thanking your boss instead."

A mischievous smile curved her lips, and it threw him off-balance. He had no idea what kind of game she was playing here, but whatever it was, he was in favor of encouraging her flirtation.

He allowed his voice to grow slightly husky. "You can still thank me, if you want to."

She responded in kind, looking up at him through the dark fringe of her lashes. "How would you like me to thank you?"

He grinned. "Orally is fine," he said matter-of-factly.

"What?" She reared back in shock.

"Someone's got a dirty mind." Shaking his head, he leaned toward her. His smile broadened. "I just meant that you could use words."

He only caught a glimpse of the color flooding her cheeks before she buried her face in her hands.

"Oh, God." She sounded endearingly, miserably muffled. "I think I need to go home now."

If the table had been smaller—and if he'd known her better—he would have cupped a reassuring hand under her jaw. But it wasn't, and he didn't, so he'd have to use words, too.

"Hey," he said. "No need for that. This has been fun."

In fact, this meal with Brenna contrasted starkly with the rest of his life, which had been nearly 100 percent devoid of anything other than work for quite some time. Then and there, Cal resolved to change that.

After he made partner.

"Haven't you had a good time?" he asked.

Her hands fell away and she looked up at him, still adorably pink-cheeked. "Up to the point when I died of mortification, yes."

"Look." He held her gaze. "We can call it a night, if that's what you want. But I'm happy to grab some coffee, or a drink, if you want to keep going." And he'd go right along with her, as long and as far as she'd let him. Even though what he *should* be doing was getting back to work. The closing argument was pretty good, but he still wanted to practice it a few more times before tomorrow morning, on the off chance the plaintiffs rested their case a day earlier than expected.

Cal was used to late nights and short sleep, though. There was no reason he couldn't spend more time with Brenna tonight and practice the closing again in the morning. Because he wanted this. He wanted *her*. She was a vision, straight out of any man's fantasies. But that wasn't the entirety of it. There was something intriguing about her, or maybe about the two of them together, that kept needling him, urging him not to simply let these few brief hours fade into memory.

She shook her head, regret turning her sensual mouth down at the corners. "I really wish I could, but I've got an early start tomorrow."

It was a disappointing response, but he of all people understood the demands of a strong work ethic. "Maybe some other time, then." Though he couldn't imagine when that other time might be. He knew he was hard up, but when had he gotten so greedy that a fantastic meal, some intriguing flirtation, and maybe a good-night kiss if he was lucky, weren't enough?

When he'd met Brenna, that's when. God help him.

He added a tip to the receipt and signed it. Then he helped her into her coat before shrugging on his own.

As they exited the restaurant, he rested a hand at the small of her back, wishing New England's spring weather were less capricious. Too many layers of fabric now kept him from sensing the play of Brenna's muscles as she walked, the warmth of her skin. It occurred to him that she'd had her hands all over his body, but he'd barely touched her. And he had no way of rectifying that imbalance.

"Where are you headed?" he asked. "Can I walk you somewhere?"

"Just to the T station."

Concerned, he spoke without thinking. "You're taking

the subway? At this hour?"

She visibly bristled. "I always do, sometimes even later than this. It's safe."

"I'd feel better if you took a cab. Let me get one for you."

"No thanks, I prefer public transit," she said coolly.

He could tell he was increasing her agitation, but he didn't feel right about dropping her off at a subway station and just walking away from her. "Look, if it's about money, I'm happy to pay for you—"

"No!" Her protest was loud and forceful. "Look, this wasn't a date, and I can get home on my own."

Her narrow-eyed glare sliced him to ribbons, and her body language told him his chances of a good-night kiss were rapidly dwindling. She'd stiffened, crossing her arms in front of her chest defensively. As much as it irked him, he needed to back off, pronto. If he didn't, she was going to walk away from him, breaking that fragile but undeniable thread of connection between them.

Cal gently touched her arm. "Hey. I'm sorry. I overstepped. I'm just used to watching out for my friends, when it's late. But you know this part of the city better than I do." His shoulders tightened. "Let me walk you to the T station?"

She paused for what seemed like eons before rendering judgment. "Okay. That would be nice." Then the humor gleamed in her eyes once more. "But no funny stuff."

He raised three fingers in a salute. "Scout's honor." Thank God she'd given him another chance.

"It's just a couple of blocks."

"Lead the way." He swept his hand forward with a

courtly gesture.

Their route took them past Newbury Street's curved and angled brick-fronted facades, each with its own set of brownstone steps. As they walked, he again drew her into a low-key conversation he hoped would defuse the tension that had built during their disagreement. He'd employed that tactic dozens of times in working with nervous witnesses, to build rapport. It seemed to meet with some success with Brenna, too, as she told him about the Indian restaurant that had been the other option she'd offered for their dinner, and he expressed his appreciation that she'd suggested Ciro's.

They stopped at the elaborate wrought-iron entrance to the station. The uneasy moment of their parting had arrived. He'd learned his lesson though, and he forced himself to let Brenna take charge.

She leaned toward him, and he bent down, not making any assumptions and deliberately allowing her to set their limits.

Soft and yielding, her lips pressed against his own.

The hunger of desire overtook him, and he fisted his hands at his sides to keep from tangling them in her hair, to keep himself from deepening their kiss, the way *he* wanted.

Instead, his eyelids fell shut as he inhaled her scent, hoping to imprint it on his memory. Something floral, jasmine maybe, mingled with the pleasant yet distinctive fragrance of the massage oil he remembered from two weeks ago.

Too soon, she pulled away. He straightened, clearing his throat, already wishing he could kiss her again.

"Good luck with your trial," she said.

"Thanks. I'll let you know how it goes."

"Bye, Cal," she said, her eyes luminous and lovely.

"Until next time." Cal hoped his confident smile masked all of his inconvenient feelings.

He watched as she descended the stairs, until she disappeared from view. His heart sank just a little when she didn't look back.

6

WITH THE IMPRINT OF CAL'S LIPS still tingling on her own, Brenna caught one last glimpse of him, still watching her as she rounded the corner of the Copley station stairway. She refused to look longingly behind her like some asinine princess parting from her swain. What would have been the point, anyway? He lived in DC and she lived in Boston, and both of them were insanely busy with their careers. Better to just make a clean break of it and walk away with her dignity intact and her head held high.

Her phone buzzed with a new text message just as she opened the door to her condo. The message was probably just from Cissy, so she made herself wait to look at it until she'd gone upstairs and gotten ready for bed. Because why bother rushing headlong toward disappointment? The longer she waited to read it, the longer she could pretend it was from Cal.

At last, she got under the covers. It was time to face reality.

But the message *was* from Cal. He'd sent her a sweet text, telling her how much he'd enjoyed their dinner. Fists in the air, she did an exultant little shimmy before realizing she had no idea how to respond, or if she even should.

Maybe Cissy could help her figure it out. It was after ten o'clock, but that wasn't especially late for a management consultant. Especially one who was waiting for her to call.

She sent Cissy a text: *Just got back from dinner with Cal.*

As expected, her phone rang less than a minute later. No greeting or other prelude, just her friend asking excitedly, "So how did the not-date go?"

"The dinner part was good. We went to Ciro's."

"Oh my God, I'm so jealous. I haven't been there in forever!"

This was one of the many reasons why Brenna loved Cissy—Cissy was undeniably successful now, but she still adored divey pizza joints and could unashamedly envy Brenna for eating at one.

"Did he pay, or did you split it?" Cissy asked.

"He expensed it, so I decided not to argue."

"Ah. And what was the not-so-good part?" Cissy didn't miss much.

"Well, he got a bit…proprietary after dinner, when I said I was going to take the T home. He wanted to pay for a cab for me, and I refused, of course. Things got kind of heated, but he backed off. Even apologized."

"So now what?"

"I don't know. Probably nothing. He doesn't live here," Brenna said, masking her disappointment.

"Where does he live?"

"DC."

"Oh come on," Cissy scoffed, "that's just a shuttle flight away. Totally doable."

"Convenient, because Cal is also totally doable." Cissy

giggled, and then snorted, and then they both started laughing in earnest. When Brenna caught her breath again, she said, "He sent me a text afterward though, and I don't know what to say. It's been forever since I've done this."

"What did the text say?"

"Just that he'd had a great time and wished he could see me again."

"Well, what do you want to happen?" the ever-practical Cissy asked. "Text him that."

"I don't know, I feel really torn."

Cissy made a fond yet exasperated noise. "Okay, then when we get off the phone, think about it, and *then* send him the text."

"Thanks for your sage advice." Brenna grinned, despite her sarcastic tone. "I'm sure I couldn't have come up with that on my own." Then she changed the subject. "So how's Ash?"

"He's good." Cissy paused before confessing, "We've been talking about moving in together when his lease is up in the fall."

"Really? That's fantastic! You guys are so good together. Are you excited?"

"I am. He already spends pretty much every night over here anyway, and it's been three years. I feel like we're ready."

"Well, keep me posted. See you Tuesday?"

"Oh, right. Mel's thing. Yeah, it's in my calendar."

Brenna could imagine Cissy's wry smile. She lived and died by her calendar. Not that Brenna was much different; her calendar just usually had a lot more blank spaces these days than Cissy's did.

"Love you, Ciss."

"Love you, too."

Brenna ended the call and immediately started thinking about how to respond to Cal's text, before her brain cells went off-line for the rest of the night. Half an hour later, she'd crafted the perfect reply.

Alas, all her wordsmithing was for naught. When she greeted her first client on Monday morning, Cal still hadn't texted her back. She'd ended up telling him she'd had a great time too, and he should let her know the next time he was in Boston.

If that turned out to be never, well then, so be it.

By the time she sent her last client on her way that night, never was looking increasingly likely. Brenna was glad she'd set her expectations low. Luckily, she was too busy to care about Cal's silence right now. She left cleanup and prep for the next morning and just headed home, still in her uniform—something she rarely did. Exhausted as she was, it couldn't be helped.

Staggering up the three seemingly endless flights of stairs to her condo, she wanted nothing more than a quick grilled cheese sandwich and a glass of juice before she passed out. For a moment, she desperately wished she had someone to make dinner for her. But all she had was herself. At times like these, that was damned depressing.

While she waited for the cheddar to melt, she checked her e-mail. Among the usual slew of messages was one Cal had sent a few hours ago. She came immediately and completely awake.

From the time stamp, he must have sent it shortly after

he'd left court that afternoon. He told her again how much he'd enjoyed seeing her and said he hoped he could get together with her again soon. Then he casually mentioned that he was going to give the closing argument for his trial tomorrow morning and invited her to come and watch. Her eyes widened. He hadn't once said anything at dinner about it, even though she knew doing a closing argument must be a pretty big deal. Confidence and modesty were such a rare, appealing combination that she once again had to temper her attraction to Cal with the knowledge that nothing was likely to come of it.

She considered his invitation. Watching the closing arguments could be interesting. She'd never been on a jury, and her only exposure to trials and courtroom scenes had been the Hollywood versions. Besides, it would probably be the last time she saw Cal, even if it was at a distance. If the closing arguments didn't run too long, she could squeeze it in—barely—before her first appointment of the day. Yawning, she decided she'd make up her mind in the morning, when her brain might possibly be functioning again.

But Cal's last few sentences provided another stimulating jolt of adrenaline:

Maybe once the trial is over, we could go out for dinner? If the jury comes back with a verdict as quickly as we're expecting, I'll probably be heading back to DC on Wednesday at the latest, though I'm in Boston pretty regularly to see my family and meet with clients. I'll definitely let you know next time I'm in town.

He apparently didn't feel as pessimistic about possibilities for the two of them as she did. Then again, it shouldn't be surprising that a guy like Cal would go after what he wanted.

She couldn't help the incredulous thrill she got from knowing that what Cal wanted was her.

BRENNA WOKE SHORTLY AFTER SUNRISE on Tuesday, feeling refreshed. She decided she could watch the closing arguments and still get to Serenity Massage in time to prepare the suite for her first client of the day. God, how she wished she'd had the energy to take care of that last night.

So just before nine o'clock, she slipped into the courtroom and sat down in the back near the doors, so she could sneak out again if she had to. She soaked in the rituals of justice, the bailiff's traditional words, the stately interior of the courtroom. The plaintiff's attorney was a woman—a pleasant surprise—though Brenna didn't find her speech particularly inspiring. Then again, Brenna would be the first to admit she was probably biased. She'd swear the ghost of Cal's kiss still lingered on her lips from Sunday night.

Cal, as expected, was incredible, even from her awkward, three-quarter profile angle most of the way across the room. Intelligent and persuasive, the man totally owned the courtroom. And he was wearing the hell out of his charcoal gray suit. She glanced at the jury now and then, and just like her, every single one of them—both the women and the men—seemed completely hooked.

Enrapt, she didn't even think to check the time until he'd finished. She was relieved it was only a few minutes after ten; she'd be fine, as long as she didn't dawdle. As the judge started instructing the jury, she crept out of the courtroom.

The subway gods were with her, and she arrived at Serenity Massage with plenty of time to freshen the suite. As she worked through her day, she kept expecting to get a text or e-mail from Cal with the verdict. But by mid-afternoon, when she was cleaning up after her last client, she still hadn't heard from him. She guessed the jury must still be out.

And now it was time to get ready for Mel's "thing," as Cissy had put it. Mel had turned thirty today, and the girls were all going out for supposedly authentic Mexican at Cantina Perla, the new tequila bar in the ultra-hip Seaport district, after Cissy got off work.

Brenna had brought a change of clothes with her, and she put them on now. A spray of pink cherry blossoms swept across the front of her form-fitting white top. Her slightly flared black skirt hit a few inches above the knee, and black boots hugged her calves like a second skin. She applied a touch of makeup before brushing out her hair until it shone, long and sleek.

Still no word from Cal by the time she arrived at the Cantina. And her phone was going to stay in her purse until she was on her way back home, so she resolved to enjoy this rare night out with her friends without thinking about him further.

Nearly a dozen women were gathered around a pair of high-top tables, with Mel in the center of it all. At least one round of shots had already been downed by the look of it, but no one was sloppy. Yet.

Over the next couple of hours they enjoyed a Mexican feast, capped by another round of shots to toast Mel's milestone birthday. Brenna had moved on to strawberry margaritas with some of the other girls and was feeling halfway to bulletproof when Cissy, who was facing the door, leaned over and said in a low, excited voice, "Hey, Mr. Super-hottie just walked in."

Brenna shrugged. There was no super-hottie hotter than Cal. Not that she was going to think about him tonight. "Don't you have a boyfriend?" Brenna reminded her.

Cissy completely ignored her. "He's looking right over here, you know."

Brenna rolled her eyes this time.

"Wait, now he's coming over here!"

Cissy's play-by-play was getting tiresome. Despite the feeling of well-being her tequila armor brought on, she wasn't in the mood to check out the so-called eye candy.

On her other side, Mel squealed drunkenly, "Oooh, you guys got me a preshent!" and Brenna finally decided she'd better see what was going on. She turned just as Cal reached her side.

"Cal! What are you doing here?"

Of all the tequila bars in the city of Boston, he had to show up here. After she'd had a few drinks. Too many emotions swirled through her, a strange mix of pleasure, surprise, and confusion rising to the top.

"Celebrating." His smile was radiant.

Even with her head buzzing, she could still put two and two together. "You won the trial! Congratulations. Though I'm not surprised after what I saw this morning."

She returned his grin, noticing for the first time that he'd changed out of his suit into light gray dress pants with a subtle plaid pattern, and a white oxford shirt, the top button enticingly open.

"So you did make it to the closing arguments! I wasn't sure, and then I didn't see you…"

"I sat at the back, in case it ran long and I needed to leave early. You were amazing, by the way."

"Thanks," he said with the same confidence he'd displayed that morning as he'd won over the jury. "I still can't believe you're here, after you didn't respond to my text when the verdict came back."

He'd texted her? "Sorry about that," she said with a rueful shrug, cursing her perfectly rational decision to shut off her phone as soon as she'd arrived.

He shook his head. "What are the odds that my pub crawl ended up at the same bar as your…birthday party?"

And that's when Brenna remembered that a tableful of tipsy women was observing this conversation. She imagined how it must appear to them—her world clearly narrowed to Cal, her friends entirely forgotten as she soaked up his every word.

Her face heated, her flush hopefully invisible in the bar's dim lighting. "Umm…my friend's birthday party. Mel—Melanie—is the birthday girl." Brenna nodded her head, indicating her dark-haired friend.

"Happy birthday," he told Mel.

Mel preened drunkenly. "Thanks! Yer pretty. I like you." She turned to Rikki, who'd given up fighting to keep a straight face. "I like 'im." She aimed a thumb in Cal's general direction.

With an impressive demonstration of self-control, Cal didn't laugh at Mel's pronouncement. Though his smile grew noticeably wider.

Brenna wanted to hide in mortification, but she womanned up instead. "I suppose I should do the honors." Then she gestured to each of her tablemates in turn as she introduced them to Cal, moving quickly around the table in hopes of avoiding further embarrassment. Finally, the moment of truth arrived. She braced herself. "Ladies, this is Cal Wilcox."

Rikki arched a brow. "Cal, your *client?*" Her friends could be so obnoxious sometimes.

"You remember. Her *former* client," Cissy corrected loyally.

Brenna eagerly jumped on the bandwagon, for the benefit of the rest of Mel's birthday guests. "Yes. My *former* client."

Said former client bent down then and murmured an apology in Brenna's ear. "Sorry to crash your party, but I saw you over here and I couldn't help myself."

She shivered as his heated breath caressed the sensitive skin behind her earlobe.

He paused there. "Mmm, you smell good." Then his lips moved south, to her neck, and unerringly found her sweet spot.

"Damn, girl," Rikki muttered, sounding envious. One of the other girls gasped—in shock or admiration Brenna couldn't tell. Then again, the blood was roaring in her ears like pounding surf. Maybe she was merely having auditory hallucinations.

"You should probably stop doing that," she said

shakily, even as she let her eyelids close, tilting her head to give Cal better access.

He hesitated. "But you like it. I can tell."

She did like it. Too much. It was her own fault for letting herself get so sex-starved, but if she let him keep it up much longer, she might have an orgasm right here in the bar, in front of all her friends.

What was she going to tell him? That she was just a few nuzzles away from coming all over the barstool? He'd probably take it as a challenge. Or maybe she should just embrace the truth—that she was tired, so fucking tired, of being hopelessly, relentlessly alone. Untouched. Un...nuzzled.

No, she most certainly did not want Cal to stop with the gentle nibbles, and the fleeting kisses, and holy crap—

His tongue-tip traced a tiny figure eight against the side of her neck. Her inner muscles responded with a slow, delicious clench as a hard shudder rippled through her. And then, before she could stifle it, a low, needy little moan managed to escape.

Brenna froze—eyes closed, neck arched, lips parted. She was so, so screwed. All she could do was pray that her friends hadn't heard how badly she wanted him.

But Cal had.

He stilled, then his voice was at her ear again, all dark and rumbly and sexy as hell. "That was just about the hottest fucking thing I've ever heard."

Scrupulously avoiding eye contact with the rest of the table, she dared to look up at him. His eyes were sex-glazed, his pupils large and dark. Miraculously, his need seemed to mirror her own.

A fierce wave of pride rolled through her. It didn't matter that she was woefully out of practice, or that everyone was undoubtedly still watching them. *She'd* put that look on his face. He wanted *her*.

Leaning toward Cal, she aimed for sultry. "Yeah, you and everyone else." Her heart was beating faster than a hummingbird's wings because of what she was about to say, and she hoped her nervousness didn't show. "Maybe we should take this somewhere more...private?" A casual suggestion, as if this wasn't far outside the bounds of her normal behavior.

That brought him up short. He nodded slowly, his eyes gleaming. "I'm on board with that. How much longer are you staying?" His words had taken on a husky urgency that sent her desire spiraling.

"What time is it?" Brenna asked no one in particular, choosing to ignore that she would never hear the end of this from Rikki and Mel.

"Time for you to get laid," one of her friends cackled.

"It's well past *that* time, if you ask me." That was Cissy. Traitor.

Brenna put her hands on her hips as she mock-glared around the table. "Seriously, guys."

"It's about nine-fifteen," Cal told her in his bedroom-iest voice.

Which meant she'd been partying for more than four hours. Even though she'd already made the suggestion to Cal, she hated being *that girl*—the one who bailed out of a girls' night to get with a guy. She was never *that girl*.

"That's my birthday preshent to you then, Brennnna." Poor Mel was slurring even more than before. "Because

yer sesh a good friend. Go wiv the seck-shee man." She
waved her hands in a shooing motion.

"Fine," Brenna acquiesced. "Majority rules! I'm outta
here."

Easing herself off the stool, she smiled at her soon-to-
be lover. Outwardly, she was all swagger. She was taking
the hottest man in the bar home with her, and every single
one of the women at the table knew it.

But inside, she was a tangled mass of nerves. Though
she knew Cal, sort of, she didn't ordinarily bring near-
strangers back to her condo. Or have one-night stands, for
that matter. Assuming she went through with it and actually slept with him, Cal was going to be her first.

"Thanks for letting me steal her," he told Mel, all gen-
tlemanly politeness. Then he bent down to Brenna's ear,
and his breath sweeping across her skin sent shivers all
the way down to her core. "Thanks for letting me steal
you." He expressed his gratitude with a kiss dropped right
onto that sensitive spot on the tendon at the side of her
neck.

Brenna's nipples tightened into hard, tingly little nubs,
and all her misgivings about leaving the party were forgotten.

Cal straightened. Then he looked down, muttering a
curse when he noticed the evidence of her arousal jutting
through her shirt's clingy fabric.

Cissy, observing all, helpfully handed Brenna her
purse, which had been hanging on the back of Brenna's
chair. Thank God for Cissy.

Brenna slung her purse over her shoulder. As she was
about to leave, Cissy took Brenna's hands in hers. "You're

sure about this—it's not just the margaritas, right?" she asked quietly.

Brenna nodded.

"Okay." Cissy gave Brenna's fingers a little squeeze. "Be safe. And call me tomorrow!" Cissy kissed her on the cheek. Then her face lit up with a playful smile. "I agree with your assessment, by the way."

Brenna's brain was still buzzing from the combined effects of tequila and heavy flirtation. "What?"

"Totally doable," Cissy said directly into her ear.

At least the remark was discreet. Nevertheless, Brenna's cheeks heated, and she couldn't escape fast enough. "Bye, everyone!"

A chorus of good-byes, with a suggestive "Have fun!" thrown in for good measure—probably by Rikki—sent them on their way.

Cal wrapped his arm around Brenna's waist as he guided her to the front of the restaurant. The heat of him seeped through the barrier of their clothes, and the cacophony of the bar faded away as her world narrowed once again to the shockingly gorgeous man at her side. She softened against him.

"Please tell me you're not drunk. Are you, Brenna?"

"No, just a little tipsy." She thought for a moment before deciding she'd better ask him the same question. "How about you?"

"Nah, I'm fine. Better than fine." He gave her a panty-melting grin. "I need a few minutes to say my own good-byes, though, before we head out."

"I need to use the ladies' anyway. Meet you at the front door in five?" she asked, as if they made plans together like this all the time.

"Sounds good." He gathered her to his side with one last squeeze. Then he let her go.

She had five minutes to stop freaking out. And find a breath mint.

7

AFTER BRENNA AND CAL RECONNECTED and emerged together from the bar, he gave her a choice. "The hotel, or your place?"

Even after a few drinks, Brenna still knew the hotel was a nonstarter. "Come to my place," she urged him. "We can go to my favorite diner for breakfast in the morning." Because Lord knew, her cupboards were bare of anything she'd want to serve him as a meal.

Then she realized what she'd assumed and quickly backpedaled. "Uh, if you're staying over, I mean." God, she sucked at this.

Cal smiled. "I can't turn down an offer like that. How do we get there?"

Relief weakened her knees. "Cab," she replied, flagging one down. "It's ten, fifteen minutes. Not much longer than going to the hotel."

He put the time to good use. As soon as they were settled in the back seat with the cabbie headed toward Charlestown, Cal hauled Brenna to him, plundering her mouth like an invading Saxon. His lips were soft yet firm, his slick tongue thrusting gently against her own. He tasted of hops and lime. *Coronas,* she thought incongruously as her insides liquefied.

Finally he broke away, panting slightly. "I've been wanting to do that for two weeks."

"Me too," she admitted, rather breathless herself.

That, apparently, was all the encouragement he needed. He pulled her toward him again, and she met him halfway, arching against him as his tongue teased hers. This time, he took it one step further. His left hand—the one against the seat back, hidden from the cabbie's view—curved around her ribcage, his thumb lightly caressing her breast.

She moaned into his mouth. This was starting to edge into dangerous territory for her again.

Maybe she could distract him. Her hand caressed its way down his side, then across his hipbone, inching ever closer to the ridge in his pants. He gasped as her fingertips trailed across the firm sponginess of that ridge's end, and he clutched her tighter.

Then his busy thumb swept along the edge of her areola, before driving right over the top of her nipple. She nearly sobbed as the sensation swamped her, wanting nothing more than to throw her leg across his lap so she could grind herself to completion.

Cal's other arm dropped down, the one she prayed had been screening his more daring activities from the cabbie. But all thoughts of self-preservation were lost when his hand gripped her thigh, then glided upward, under the hem of her skirt. Her legs parted, just enough for his questing fingers to home in on where she was hot and damp with excitement. His fingertips brushed against her swollen folds through her panties, and she almost lost it, right there.

Now her every exhalation was pretty much a moan, and she no longer gave a shit whether the cabbie saw her have the orgasm of her life in his back seat.

The taxi lurched to a stop, and the dome light over their heads came on. Was the driver throwing them out for practically having sex in his cab? Disoriented, she regarded him anxiously in the rearview mirror.

He leered back at her. "Twelve dollars."

Cal frowned. "You go ahead. I've got this."

Still dazed, Brenna got out while Cal lingered to pay the fare. He came up behind her as she was fumbling her keys out of her purse.

She unlocked the door to her building, and he held it open as she walked through. "Third-floor walk-up. Sorry," she warned him as she began to ascend the stairs ahead of him.

"Not a problem," he assured her, sliding a hand up under her skirt and giving her right cheek a little squeeze.

She thought about protesting for form's sake. Instead, she just upped her pace the rest of the way to the top.

With trembling hands, she unlocked her apartment door. Then Cal was on her, kicking the door closed behind them, finally pressing her against the wall.

"I need to make you come." His breathing was as fast and ragged as her own.

"Mmm hmm," she agreed, quickly losing herself again in the bright spears of lust shooting through her as his hand burrowed inside her panties, two of his long fingers delving into her slick and needy hole.

Too soon, he dropped to his knees in front of her, pulling her panties down as he went. She drew her skirt up with one hand. The other curved around the back of his head, his hair soft against her fingertips.

Mesmerized, she watched as he leaned in, inhaling long and deeply. Then his tongue darted out to taste her.

Brenna let out a heated sigh of approval. "I'm already close." She barely recognized her own voice, hoarsened with desire.

He suckled her clit between warm, firm lips, strumming it with his tongue. "Oh my God!" she cried out, her hips bucking involuntarily against his face.

When he slid his fingers back inside her, a dozen long, sweeping licks was all it took to topple her over the edge. She climaxed, thrashing and moaning, against his tongue and hand.

If it weren't for the wall at her back, she would have collapsed into a contented little heap. She sagged against its cool solidity, trying to remember how to breathe. If the *foreplay* was that good, the main event just might kill her.

Almost reverently, Cal skimmed Brenna's panties the rest of the way down, over her boots, and steadied her as she stepped out of them. Then he stood up, wiping the back of his hand across his shining mouth and chin. The intent in his eyes was unmistakable.

Bracing one hand against the wall, he toed off his shoes and nudged them aside. He stepped back to unbuckle his belt and unzip his trousers, pulling a strip of six condoms from one of his pockets as his pants fell to his ankles.

Brenna's indrawn breath caught in her lungs. This was really happening.

Cal kicked his pants toward his shoes. Then he pushed

his boxers down until they dropped to the floor, where they soon joined the growing pile. The tip of his erection poked between his white shirttails.

"You come prepared, I see," Brenna teased as she caressed his hardness. His rather well-endowed hardness. "Boy Scout?"

"Eagle Scout," he corrected her with a playful smile. He tore off one of the packets, ripped it open, and sheathed himself. "Ready?"

"Oh, yeah."

Before she knew what was happening, he'd hoisted her up, his hands gripping the curves of her ass. Instinctively, her arms came around his neck, her legs around his waist. He held her in place, adjusting their positions until his crown was poised at her entrance. Then he allowed gravity to impale her on his erection in one slow, delicious glide.

"Fuck," they gasped almost in unison when her body had finally come to rest against his. She was stuffed absolutely full of him.

He started to move, bouncing her on his cock, jolting her against the wall with each stroke. "You feel incredible," Cal said with a groan before plunging into her again.

Brenna couldn't even find the words to respond coherently. The way his pubic bone rubbed against her clit, combined with the way he filled her as he advanced, then retreated, rendered her damn near speechless.

Cal picked up the pace, mercilessly pounding into her eager body. The delicious ache of another orgasm soon began to twine and coil inside her, growing in intensity.

"Oh, Cal!" Her body bowed as she cried out, the

tension peaking before she finally tumbled over the edge of ecstasy. Her eyelids fell shut, her inner muscles clasping him in a series of intense, shuddering pulses.

"Thank God," she barely heard him mutter through the roaring in her ears. "Didn't think I was gonna make it." His thrusts grew even rougher. Within seconds he was choking out her name as he seemed to stagger.

Still stunned, Brenna forced her heavy lids open, trying to get her bearings. The first thing she saw was Cal in the throes of his orgasm, his eyes practically rolling back in his head. Even better than she'd imagined. Especially the way he was shoving his cock extra deep inside her as he came.

Cal's sweaty forehead dropped to her shoulder. It got her no end of hot that he was strong enough to keep her pinned to the wall, even after he'd just set her world spinning around a new axis. But, sooner than she really wanted, he bent his knees, gently pulling out of her before he lowered her to the floor.

"Are you okay?" he asked in a voice hoarsened by his exertions. "I wasn't too rough, was I?"

"God, no." She hastened to reassure him. "You were perfect. It was incredible."

He smiled down at her, tenderly tracing her jaw with his fingertips. "For me, too."

The moment of perfection was all too fleeting, though. Her overactive brain kicked in, and a sudden jolt of anxiety evaporated most of her postorgasmic haze. Were they supposed to make idle chitchat between rounds? Should she give him a tour of her apartment? She supposed she should offer him a drink, at least.

Cal must have realized that her mind was starting to race out of control—or maybe he was just a master of timing—because he took swift and confident action. He enfolded her in his arms, pulling her close for a long and luxurious kiss. By the time they came up for air, all of her fears, all of her nervousness, all of the what-ifs had just drifted away, dispersed by his comforting warmth and masculine scent.

"I could kiss you like that all night," he said in a low and husky rumble.

"Mmm...more kisses?" she pleaded wistfully.

He chuckled. "Maybe somewhere more comfortable?"

Yeah, kisses in bed sounded pretty darned good. Preferably with less clothing, and more horizontality. "Let me just get a couple glasses of water for us and we can head upstairs."

He removed the condom, careful not to spill its contents. "Do you have a bathroom somewhere I can trash this?"

"Yeah. Sure. It's just down that hallway, on the right." She pointed, and he nodded in acknowledgment.

While he dealt with the condom, she unzipped her boots and tugged them off, lining them up in the front hall closet and stashing Cal's shoes alongside them. Her panties peeked out from underneath his trousers. Lacking a pocket to tuck them into, she decided to put them back on. Then she headed for the kitchen.

A few minutes later she rejoined Cal, now barefoot and wearing just his shirt. He'd folded his slacks across his arm and was holding his boxers and socks in his other hand. She assumed he'd collected the rest of the condoms—they were nowhere to be seen.

She took a deep breath, then released it. They had water. They had condoms. There was a bed waiting for them upstairs.

And she had a three-year dry spell to make up for. With the hottest guy she'd ever known.

She was glad he couldn't see the giddy smile that spread across her face as she led the way up to her bedroom.

BRENNA'S INTERNAL ALARM CLOCK woke her at sunrise. She was about to throw back the covers to attend to her parched throat and bursting bladder when it finally registered: the heavy weight of an arm was slung possessively across her lower belly. Soft, crinkly hair tickled her hip.

She froze mid-movement. Cal was still here. In her bed. With her.

Her heartbeat sped up as memories from last night came flooding back. She hadn't known sex could be so...intense. So all-consuming. Especially not in the context of a casual hook-up, or whatever this was.

Round two had sent them off to sleep in a blissful tangle of sweaty limbs. She'd roused Cal several hours later, or maybe he'd roused her, and they'd continued where they'd left off, sleepily joining together until both were sated once again.

And now she would have to extricate herself without waking him. The last few weeks had undoubtedly been stressful for him, and they'd barely slept last night. She was sure he needed as much rest as he could get. Besides, she had no idea what to say to him if he woke up.

Not daring to breathe, she eased herself back toward the edge of the bed, gently setting his arm down into the still-warm hollow where she'd lain.

Frowning, he made a drowsy noise of complaint, but didn't stir.

She rolled to her feet, trying not to shift the bed-springs, and noticed for the first time precisely which underused muscles had gotten a workout last night. Her legs trembled like a newborn fawn's as she made her way to the bathroom. But a big drink of water and a couple of ibuprofen went a long way toward setting her right. As did a thorough tooth-brushing.

She didn't know what the standard protocol was, so she left a spare toothbrush on the counter for whenever Cal woke up. And the Advil, in case his head felt anything like hers did.

Ablutions completed, she stood next to her bed for a few minutes, greedily drinking in the sight of gorgeous, sandy-haired Cal felled by sleep. He looked several years younger, with his muscles relaxed and the fringes of his brown lashes lying in twin crescents against his cheeks. The dusting of freckles across his nose made her imagine what he'd looked like as a boy. But even in repose he was all man, powerful and sensual.

She shivered in the morning chill and decided coffee could wait a little longer. Right now, all she wanted was to slide back under the covers, snuggle up next to Cal's warmth, and catch a couple more hours of sleep herself. Thankfully she'd planned ahead, expecting to be exhausted after Mel's party, and her first massage appointment today wasn't until noon.

It was surprisingly easy to relax against him, her head pillowed on his chest as it slowly rose and fell. His skin was smooth and firm against her cheek. She shifted onto her side, tentatively sliding her hand around his waist.

It had been amazing, and weird, to wake up next to someone after so long on her own. She suppressed a sigh as her heavy eyelids closed. Might as well soak up as much comfort as she could, while she could, before she was once more flying solo. Because in just a few short hours, that's exactly what she'd be doing.

She woke again when Cal slipped into bed behind her.

"Thanks for the toothbrush," he murmured, greeting her with mint-scented kisses along her jaw.

"Mmm. You're welcome." She stretched languorously, and Cal paused in his attentions. "Keep kissing," she commanded him, still drowsy.

He ignored her request, nuzzling his way down her neck instead and setting off cascades of delicious shivers. "So." His breath puffed against her ear. "I was looking at your shower, and it gave me an idea."

"What kind of idea?"

"The kind of idea that's better as a show than a tell."

As she soon learned, it was the kind of idea that involved warm water coursing over their slick bodies during an exquisitely slow round four.

Cal had the best ideas.

They eventually got dressed, with plenty of time for her to take him to breakfast as she had promised. He was overdressed in yesterday's trousers and white oxford—the guys' version of a walk of shame—but she was still proud to show him off at her favorite neighborhood diner.

Over coffee, toast, and omelets, she admitted something she hadn't gotten the chance to tell him last night. "I don't usually do…this, you know."

"What, eat breakfast?"

His smile sent a rush of lust through her, even while his wisecrack made her roll her eyes.

"No," she huffed at him.

"One-night stands?" he asked in a lower, more sympathetic voice.

"Is that what this is?" Even though she'd thought it herself, it was surprisingly painful to hear him say it.

"Not if you don't want it to be. I'd like to see you again."

Now, *that* was unexpected. "But you don't live here."

His response was pretty much the same as Cissy's had been. "DC isn't that far away. I could come up on weekends. If you're not working," he added hastily.

"You'd really do that?" She couldn't quite believe it would be so easy to resolve the long-distance thing.

"Are you kidding me?" His volume had risen, and he lowered it, leaning across the table. "Last night, and this morning, was by far the best sex I've ever had. I am absolutely in favor of as many repeats as possible."

"Oh." She tried to hide her disappointment behind a joke. "So it'd be a multi-night stand then."

"I prefer to think of it as friends-with-benefits."

He sounded so fucking reasonable when he said it, but the concept still made her heart hurt. They didn't know each other well enough to be friends, so what did that make them, exactly?

"I haven't actually done that before, either. Would either of us have any other 'friends' we share 'benefits' with?"

He frowned. "I'd rather we didn't."

Well, she'd rather they pursued a romantic relationship and not just some bullshit casual sex thing, but it didn't look like that was in the cards. It was going to be this, or nothing.

Ordinarily she would have opted for the latter, but her newly fledged wanton side took the opportunity to remind her how spectacular last night had been. It had been by far the best sex she'd ever had, too. She'd just been hoping for the possibility of more, if they were going to bother continuing to see each other in the first place.

Maybe she could be a big girl and seize this chance to push her boundaries. Maybe the friends-with-benefits thing would work better than her instincts suggested. She was still ridiculously busy. Realistically, she had no time to pursue a serious relationship right now anyway. Not until her business was stable, and who knew when that would be. She shouldn't be surprised that Cal wasn't interested in something serious either. At least he was being up front about it, and he wanted to be monogamous.

"Okay," she said, convincing herself. Mostly. She could do this.

His face lit up like he'd just been given a labradoodle puppy for Christmas. "Can I come up this weekend, or are you busy?"

"Let me check my schedule." She was pleased that she sounded calm, despite the state of her nerves. She pulled out her phone and opened her calendar. "Nothing Friday night. Five appointments on Saturday, but I'm done by four o'clock or so. Two on Sunday, done by twelve-thirty." Then she looked at him. "But if someone else wants to make a booking, I need to accept it."

"Ah." He thought for a moment. Then he said, "I can work with that."

"You can?"

He nodded.

"You don't have piles of laundry to do, or groceries to buy after you've been camped out in a hotel up here for a few weeks?"

"Sure. But I can take care of all of that tonight." Thereby answering her unasked question about when he was heading back.

He pulled out his phone and tapped at it for a minute. "If I take the seven-thirty shuttle on Friday, I can be up here by a little after nine. Is that too late for you?"

"No, that's fine," she answered, bemused. Basically, they were making an appointment to have sex. Then Cal would go back on Sunday night or something, and maybe he'd come up again the following weekend for more of the same. It was bizarre how businesslike the whole arrangement was turning out to be. But if that's how it was done, she supposed she could go along with it.

"And then I could take a seven o'clock return flight on Sunday. Or eight, if you wanted to grab dinner first."

"Either way," she said faintly.

He looked up from his phone. "Hey. You sure you're okay with this?"

She dodged his question. "You seem awfully sure that you are."

Cal shrugged. "Shuttle flights are easy to change. So if it all gets too weird for you, just tell me, and I can head back early." Then he grinned at her, confidence firmly back in place. "I don't think that'll happen, though."

Well, that made one of them. Brenna was reserving judgment.

"So. Should I book these flights?"

"Sure," she said, sounding far more decisive than she felt. Maybe Cal could fuck the worries right out of her. And even if not, she ought to have some fun trying.

8

BRENNA PACED. OR MAYBE FLITTED, like the butterflies in her stomach. She settled onto her living room sofa, once again trying to relax with visualization exercises and meditation.

Her mind refused to clear. It doggedly kept returning to the train of thought dominating her brain ever since she'd left Serenity Massage earlier in the evening. *Cal will be here soon.*

And now soon was down to mere minutes. He'd texted about twenty minutes ago, after his flight had landed at Logan airport. There was nothing in her apartment left to clean, fold, or put away. She'd already showered, shaved everything that needed shaving, plucked, moisturized, painted her toenails, brushed her teeth (twice), and lightly dabbed scent onto her pulse points. A floaty floral cotton sundress revealed her shoulders and skimmed her knees in a comfortable, feminine way. The pale pink strapless bra and thong underneath probably wouldn't stay on long anyway.

She stood abruptly, needing to dissipate some of the nervous energy coursing through her body. Before she could start pacing again, the buzzer rang. She flinched at the harsh sound.

Attempting to calm her racing heart with deep-bellied breaths, she stepped over to the intercom. An unsteady finger depressed the "talk" button.

"Hi."

"Hey, it's Cal." Even the tinny voice emerging from the speaker sounded self-assured.

"I'll buzz you up."

Adrenaline coursed through her veins as she moved to the front door. She opened it a crack before deciding it might be more welcoming to wait for him on the landing so she could hold the door for him.

His footsteps grew louder as he climbed the stairs, and she soon caught a glimpse of his broad shoulders and sandy hair between the balusters. Her heart banged so hard in her chest she swore he'd be able to see it. Then he turned at the landing below and looked up.

When he saw her waiting for him, he smiled that radiant smile, the one that let her know everything was going to be all right. And if it wasn't, then he would fix it.

She couldn't help but smile back. In her anxiety, she'd forgotten just how beautifully put together he was. As he closed the distance between them, it all came rushing back.

"Hi," she said again, not caring this time how breathless she sounded.

Cal stopped one step from the top, within kissing distance. "It's good to see you. You look fantastic." His baritone rumble stroked her nerve endings like a caress.

He looked fantastic too, in flat-front khakis and a button-down shirt with the sleeves rolled up above his sculpted forearms. "Thanks. So do you."

But she still wasn't quite able to make herself bridge the gap and let herself be kissed. Cal was the more experienced partner in this dance. He'd have to lead. Though she had a feeling she'd willingly follow him just about anywhere, at least as far as bedroom-type activities were concerned.

She invited him in, and he set his bags down in the foyer. "Shoes off?" he asked.

Her own feet were already bare. She nodded, pleased.

He turned down her offer of food, but gladly accepted one of the fancy wheat beers she'd bought just for the occasion. She poured herself a companionable glass of wine—Lord knew she could use one.

As they sipped, she stood in front of him in her spotless kitchen, hoping to hell things would get significantly less awkward soon. Even amazing sex wasn't worth this sustained anxiety that she'd do something dumb and he'd decide he wasn't interested in her anymore. Or *he'd* do something dumb and make her regret she'd brought him home in the first place.

She needn't have worried, though; Cal had it covered. He started off, as he often seemed to do, with uncomplicated conversation—about the rest of her week, about the Red Sox, about the case he'd started working on almost as soon as he'd set foot in the office the previous day. The man turned *easy to talk to* into an art form.

He finished his beer, rinsed the bottle in the kitchen sink, and, like the perfect guest, asked where her recycling bin was. Then he suggested she give him the full tour of her place, which reminded her in a flash of heat how they'd spent most of their time during his first visit.

Brenna relaxed in increments as she led Cal from the kitchen into the small dining area. "I bought the condo about six years ago. It had been on the market for ages because it needed a lot of updating." In half a dozen steps, they were back in her living room. "The dining and living rooms used to have this gross wall-to-wall carpeting, but I pulled it up, and my dad and I refinished the floors." Which were wide pine and beautiful, if she said so herself.

Cal raised an eyebrow. "Hidden talents."

"You don't know the half," she said suggestively, already starting to feel more sure of herself. No tequila necessary. "The only thing the previous owners renovated was the master bath. I'm guessing they blew most of their budget on the heated floors and all that marble, and then they ran into financial troubles and gave up."

"That bathroom's incredible."

"Well, I can't take any credit for it. But even though I love it, it's not how I would've spent my money."

She looked down the hallway from her living room. "You've already seen the powder room. The laundry's under the stairs." And she felt calm enough now to suggest that they grab his bags and bring them upstairs before continuing the tour. His free hand found its way into hers as they started their climb.

At the top, they stopped first in the guest bedroom, which doubled as an office. After a brief glimpse of the bathroom next door, she led him into the master suite and dropped his laptop bag onto the armchair. He deposited his overnight bag next to it, on the floor.

She'd painted her bedroom a pale straw color and decorated it with framed Art Deco posters, which complemented the clean lines of her Mission-style furniture. A vintage *obi* in gold and forest green silk served as a runner atop her dresser, and a succulent jade plant rested in a metal stand underneath the skylight in the cathedral ceiling.

Normally, being in this room gave her a feeling of peaceful focus. But the usual effect was absent today. Because soon—if she didn't chicken out—she and Cal would be having sex. Right there, where she'd turned back the bedspread to reveal the highest thread-count sheets she owned.

Shyness bloomed once again, and she forced herself to brazen through it. "You've already seen this room, too." She pitched the words low and velvety, hoping she sounded seductive.

His voice was rich and dark like chocolate. "I hope you'll forgive me for not paying more attention to it—then, and now." He tugged gently on her hand, bringing her closer to his dizzying scent and all those firm, unyielding muscles.

Her heart was rocketing out of her chest as she turned her face upward. His kiss was so light she barely felt it at first. Like the brushing of a butterfly's wings, his lips skimmed against hers, again and again. Her lips parted, and they shared one inhalation, one exhalation before her tongue-tip tentatively entered his mouth.

He tasted of spearmint, overlaid with the Hefeweizen he'd drunk earlier. She wondered if, despite the outward show of confidence, he'd been nervous about tonight, too. He'd made sure he was ready for her, the same way she'd done for him. No five o'clock shadow scraped her face as their kiss deepened. Whatever cologne he was wearing smelled freaking amazing. His heartbeat thudded fast but steady where their bodies pressed against each other.

Unexpectedly, she found herself wanting to reassure him. To tell him that she appreciated the care he'd taken. That she was glad he hadn't rushed things when he first got here, but she was eager to get things started now. More than eager.

Her nervous anticipation heightened her senses, and now she could feel *everything*. The bulge of his arousal against her hip. His big, warm hands sliding to the small of her back, bowing her slightly as he pulled her against him. The flex of his shoulders and biceps as he surrounded her with his embrace.

She wanted to tell him all of this, but all that came out of her mouth was a sigh of pleasure. She shifted the angle of their bodies, sandwiching his erection against her belly.

He groaned before breaking their kiss. "Ah, you're getting me so hot. I wanted to take it slow…"

His tone bordered on petulant, and she had to suppress a smile. The truth was, his imminent loss of control just made her desire coil even tighter. "You can take it slow next time. Practice makes perfect, after all," she teased him. Then she took advantage of the barely perceptible gap between them to slide her thong down, over her hips, until it dropped to the floor. Along with Cal's jaw, when the scrap of pale pink lace and silk landed next to his foot.

But he recovered fast. "In that case," he said, hustling her backward to the bed, "let's get you up here."

Her dress billowed as she fell back, bunching

underneath her waist. She was about to wriggle farther onto the bed when he placed a hand on her thigh. "Stay there. I want to make sure you're ready."

"I am ready," she protested.

Kneeling beside the bed, he bent his head to her. He proceeded to thoroughly test her readiness until she was breathless and mewling, her hands grasping and clutching at the sheets.

"Mmm," he finally hummed against her sensitive bud, like she was the sweetest delicacy he'd ever tasted. Then he pushed himself upright. "Now you're ready. Let's get that dress off of you."

She sat up, a fistful of her dress in each hand. With a provocative look from beneath his light brown eyelashes, Cal withdrew a strip of condoms from his pants pocket and laid them on the bed. Then he started unbuttoning his shirt. His firm pecs and delicious abs were so distracting she froze, her dress halfway off.

He'd tossed his shirt onto the armchair in the corner and had started on his belt when he caught her staring. The hint of cockiness in his lopsided smile was far sexier than it ought to have been.

"You're a tremendous boost to my ego, you know that?" he said.

Brenna pulled her dress the rest of the way up, leaving it over her head an extra moment or two to hide her flaming cheeks. Then it was off, and she leaned back on one hand, twisting to fling it in the general direction of the chair.

When she faced him again, wearing nothing but her pale pink lacy strapless bra, Cal's expression had turned predatory. Even more so after the bra came off, too. Gratifyingly, his stripping off the remainder of his clothes became more about speed and less about putting on a show for her.

He picked up a foil packet and tore it open.

She sat up. "I want to do it." Then she leaned forward and pressed a kiss to his glistening crown for emphasis.

"Be my guest," he said, handing her the condom. His husky voice struck an answering chord low in her belly.

He watched as she unrolled it down his shaft. His cock twitched once, twice, beneath her gliding fingertips.

"Scoot back," he said, nodding toward the headboard. Then he followed her onto the bed, his hands coming to rest on either side of her ribcage and his knees pressing against her inner thighs.

She hooked her calves across his gloriously firm ass, opening herself to him. He supported himself with one hand as he guided his erection into her with the other. Then that hand dropped back to the mattress and he looked down at her, the pupils like inky pools in his gray eyes.

"I've been thinking of this since I left on Wednesday." He slid home in one sure thrust.

Her eyelids fell shut as she savored the sensation of their joining. She brought her knees up along his sides and dug her heels into his butt as it flexed taut.

"Please," was all she could say.

Bending down, he covered one of her jutting nipples with his hot mouth. She moaned, arching into the sensation as she sifted her fingers through his unexpectedly soft hair. He suckled harder, drawing on the tip of her breast again and again as he drove into her with long, even strokes. Each tug of his lips sent a corresponding jolt of desire arrowing through her.

Cal soon switched to her other breast, giving it the same careful attention. Her need for him grew, and her grip tightened on his broad shoulders.

"Greedy," he murmured against her skin as he slid a fingertip down her belly, through her dark curls, and eventually brought it to rest against her throbbing clit. His tongue, meanwhile, resumed its swirls and flicks against her pearled nipple, and his questing fingertip began to circle gently.

Brenna bucked her hips toward him as he expertly tormented her overwrought little bundle of nerves. "C'mon, Cal."

But the infuriating man was taking it slowly after all. His pace remained unhurried as he brought her higher and higher, the pleasure building within her aching core.

She tugged at him with her fingertips, urging him upward until their lips met. That seemed to catalyze him, finally, and her tongue slid into the welcoming cavern of his mouth in time with his increasingly forceful thrusts.

The gentle fluttering of his tongue against hers seemed to go straight to the tightly-puckered points of her nipples. She broke their kiss to whimper, "Oh, I'm getting close."

Her confession seemed to spur him on. He slid one hand beneath her, his palm cupping her ass as he began to power into her. His pubic bone tweaked her clit with each grinding stroke. "You gonna come?" he managed to say. "I'm real close. C'mon."

She tightened and slickened around him in response to the heady combination of his words and the indescribable feeling of him inside her.

"Ohhhh," she moaned at the same time as he gritted out, "Shit, can't stop it. I'm coming, Brenna!"

And then she was falling over the edge with him, her body detonating around him. "Ahhh!" she shouted as she writhed against him, clutching at his back and shoulders. Wave after wave of her orgasm rolled through her, overwhelming in its intensity. Cal was buried so deep inside her it felt like they couldn't possibly get any closer. Yet she craved even more.

She clung to him, and he shuddered every so often as yet another wavelet crested within her, her inner muscles rippling around his cock. Slowly, the tide ebbed, and she went limp, relishing his weight pressing her into the mattress.

Too soon, he stirred. Then he rolled to his side, still cradling her against his sweat-dampened chest. In this moment, it was difficult to remember he wasn't her boyfriend. Until she'd met Cal, she'd never slept with a man she hadn't been in love with. But even though they'd burned up the sheets, it was only sex, pure and simple.

She'd just have to keep reminding herself of that. Repeatedly. Until it stuck.

FOR BREAKFAST THE NEXT MORNING, Brenna brought Cal out to the roof deck, since they'd missed it on last night's tour. They drank coffee and ate muffins, he in low-slung pajama pants and a T-shirt, she in black yoga pants and a baby tee with Serenity Massage's stylized lotus flower silk-screened across the front.

"I like this bower you've got going on up here." He nodded at the greenery surrounding them. "It's very peaceful."

"Thanks. It'll be even greener in a couple of months, once the tomatoes and cucumbers come in." Her herb boxes along the roof deck's railings were already starting to flourish, she was pleased to note, and a profusion of blossoms and foliage spilled from her two small container gardens. "Hey, that reminds me."

He looked at her, an unspoken question on his face as he waited for her to continue.

"I owe you a snake plant."

"Now, there's a sentence you don't hear every day." He chuckled, and she joined in.

"Remember the plant I told you about that's almost impossible to kill? It's a *sansevieria*. I've got one downstairs, and I potted some cuttings from it a couple of months ago. I can pack one up to send home with you."

"I promise I'll try my best to keep it alive." His words were solemn, but laughter danced in his eyes.

"It's easy. Not too much sunlight, water it once a week or so, and it'll be fine."

"Thanks. That's very sweet of you." His gaze tangled with hers, slow and sticky like honey.

Brenna's breath caught, and she glanced away from the heat in his eyes before it scorched her. The man was insatiable. And though she'd been trying not to think about it, she needed to leave for work soon. If she didn't have a business to save, she'd stay in bed with him the whole day and glut herself on incredible sex. At least they still had tonight and most of tomorrow.

Flustered, she sipped from her mug, knowing he was still watching her. "What are you going to do today?" she asked, looking across the rooftops down to the masts of the USS *Constitution* docked in the Navy Yard.

"The firm has an office in the Financial District. I was thinking I'd walk over there and get some work done while you were out. Maybe buy a few things, so I can make you dinner tonight."

She turned back to him. "Really?" She tried to keep all traces of her soaring heart out of her expression, though even she could hear the excitement evident in that single word.

"Sure," he said. "You eat fish, don't you?" His only tell was a tiny quirk of the lips. He'd kick her ass at poker, that was for sure.

"Yeah, I love seafood." Her grin stretched stupidly from ear to ear.

After last night, she'd already been thinking he was pretty close to perfect. This revelation that he could cook, too, elevated him to demigod status after so many months of pasta with red sauce, grilled cheese sandwiches, and simple casserole dishes.

"Great. What time will you be back here?"

"Around five?"

"Okay, I'll plan to be back here around then, too."

"Okay." She sighed happily, pleased at yet another sign he wanted this weekend to go well. That he wanted to impress her. How amazing would it be to have a home-cooked meal prepared by one of the sexiest men she'd ever met?

With perks like these, this friends-with-benefits thing had way more appeal than she'd expected. Maybe once they knew each other better, if they continued to get on as well they had so far, they might consider pursuing a deeper relationship.

She could always hope.

9

BRENNA WAS IRRESISTIBLE. That's what it came down to.

Their first weekend had gotten off to a rockier start than Cal had anticipated, but by the end of it, she'd actually looked disappointed when he'd left for the airport. And the sex, in a word, had been mind-blowing.

By their second weekend, they'd already settled into sort of a routine. One that involved five or six billable hours a day at the office (for him), some number of hours at work (for her), and an unprecedented amount of time wrapping their naked bodies around each other. He refused to think about the men she might be massaging while she was on the clock, the lucky bastards.

Their third weekend together, she'd suggested he borrow her spare set of keys when he was visiting her. A suggestion he imagined she'd make to a friend staying in that combination guest room-office she'd decorated in relaxing seashore colors. He'd been oddly touched by the trust this small gesture demonstrated.

Even after just these few short weeks, he found himself wanting to do things purely for the joy they'd bring her. One time, on a whim, he picked up a bouquet of sunflowers from the open-air farmer's market he passed on his way back from the office to her place. He couldn't remember ever making someone beam the way Brenna had when he'd given it to her.

So the next time he'd walked by the market, he'd bought a punnet of fresh raspberries for dessert. And a pint of vanilla bean Häagen Dazs at the corner store. Her blissful enjoyment of them had been a thing of beauty to watch. And her tangy-sweet kisses afterward had sparked some ideas about more creative uses for ice cream.

After a month and a half, he could definitively say this was nothing like his previous friends-with-benefits relationships. He'd never cuddled with those women. There had been no second and third rounds between the sheets, no waking up together and sharing breakfast. No flowers, no dinners. This...whatever it was with Brenna, was veering wildly off course into uncharted waters.

And it concerned him. Cal didn't have time for the distraction of a girlfriend right now, especially a long-distance one. Not with the partnership decision looming over him.

Even worse, why did she have to be a massage therapist, of all things? Not that he hadn't appreciated the spectacular scalp rub she'd given him a couple of weeks ago while he'd been reviewing a junior associate's research memo. But he worried that her profession might come across as unseemly to some of the partners who would soon be voting him in—or out.

The partners didn't need much reason to say no. The economy hadn't bounced back yet from the recession, and even at the best of times, fewer than five percent of associates were given the nod.

He had to be one of them. Failure was not an option.

Not just because he'd worked hard in law school and even harder during his eight years at the firm. Not even because he respected his colleagues, loved his job—despite the crazy hours—and generally appreciated his clients.

When his father died nearly six years ago after losing a valiant battle against cancer, Cal had vowed to do whatever it took to become a partner at CMH. His hours had been above average before then, but after his father's death, Cal had become one of the firm's highest billing associates. Even though his father had worked at a smaller firm, making partner at CMH would honor his dad's memory and cement a lifelong and unbreakable connection to the man whose loss he still felt—not just as a father, but as a mentor and friend.

So he wasn't going to throw away the past decade and a half of blood, sweat, and tears, for a girl. Not even one who made him desperate for Friday to arrive each week, just so he could see her again.

No, it was better not to get too emotionally involved. He needed to stick to the straight and narrow of the partnership track and try to keep things with Brenna firmly in the friends-with-benefits category. That's why he was revising a brief on Saturday night, instead of sitting with her on the sofa and employing the scientific method to determine the most effective distraction from her chick flick.

He didn't realize she'd eased behind him until she started massaging his neck and shoulders.

"Oh, Christ. Right there." His head lolled forward as she dug into the pair of knots between his shoulder blades.

"Whatcha working on?" she asked, pressing and tugging on his tense muscles.

"Brief for a preliminary injunction," he murmured.

She tended to him in silence for a minute, apparently while reading over his shoulder, because her next question was just about the last thing he expected her to ask. "Someone violated a non-solicitation clause?"

His head came up, and he swiveled to face her. "Uh-huh," he said slowly, observing her expression. "You weren't a lawyer before becoming a massage therapist, were you?"

She stepped around to his side and backed away a pace or two, her hands in a white-knuckled clasp. "No. Not a lawyer."

"But you were something, weren't you." It wasn't even a question.

An unexpected bitterness laced her tone. "Yes. I was *something*." Her chest rose with a deep breath. Then she dropped a bombshell. "I used to be a management consultant. With McKinsey."

He must have looked like a carp on a fishhook, mouth opening and closing with no sound coming out. "Wh—what?" he finally managed. "Wow. That's…impressive."

"Yup. I'm a Stanford grad who washed out of McKinsey to become a financially struggling massage therapist."

Cal ignored the dare in her sarcastic words, too busy getting irrationally pissed off that she'd withheld all this information from him. He launched himself up, out of the chair. "Wait—you went to *Stanford*? Where I went to law school? And you never said anything?"

She took another step backward. "That's right. Not that you ever asked."

Okay. She had a point, but… "Why didn't you tell me

before?"

Crap. That had sounded way too pouty. He folded his arms across his chest, waiting.

She mirrored his gesture. "It wasn't relevant. Does it matter where the woman you're sleeping with went to college? Or how she used to earn a living?"

He wasn't touching those queries with a ten-foot pole. Struggling to keep his tone even, he instead answered her questions with one of his own. "So, why tell me now?"

She waited a beat before answering. "Because I wanted you to know."

There was something he was missing here. Something she still wasn't saying. "But *why* did you want me to know?"

Another pause, before her gaze slid away. Her voice was softer, sadder this time. Resigned in a way that made the hair on the back of his neck stand up. "Because maybe I'm getting tired of not mattering."

Well, shit.

This moment—right here, right now—might well be the first step on the path to career ruin. Yet at the same time, it was unavoidable. He'd be the biggest asshole in the world if he put his own needs first and just let her keep feeling that way. Lonely. Worthless. Like he was only interested in her for sex. When his overpowering desire to comfort her told him that wasn't true.

"Hey." He opened his arms to her. There had to be a way to walk this tightrope without falling into the abyss. "C'mere."

She hesitated before allowing him to draw her into his embrace. Her reluctance gut-punched him.

He inhaled the scent that was uniquely hers, before pressing a kiss to the crown of her head. "Of course you matter."

She heaved out a sigh against his chest, her slender arms tightening around his waist. "Look. I get that we still don't know each other all that well. But since we started this thing, we haven't even tried to talk about anything important to either of us."

Cal didn't have to think about it very long to know she was right. They'd mainly talked about innocuous things like work anecdotes, the Red Sox, current events, where to eat dinner. She'd asked about his family once, but he'd quickly changed the topic to something else. Anything to keep her from getting under his skin.

"And I know you want to keep things casual," she continued. "But I don't know if I'm wired that way."

He froze, then resumed stroking down the narrow taper of her back, her hair rubbing like raw silk against his fingertips. He'd been kidding himself earlier when he'd thought they could remain friends-with-benefits, given how they both seemed to be feeling. Although he had no idea how else to categorize what they were to each other.

One thing he was sure of, though. "I'd be lying if I said you were only a casual fling at this point."

They stood like that, holding each other, letting the meaning of each other's words sink in. Then she turned her head, pressing her forehead against his chest. His shirt muffled her next question. "So, what do we do now?"

"I don't know," he said. "Keep seeing each other, see where it goes?"

That could work, if he could finesse the timing. A slow

build with Brenna until the partnership decision was announced a few months from now. Given how the two of them had started off, it probably made sense to spend some time getting to know each other better anyway. No need to tell anyone he was dating a massage therapist while they were still figuring things out.

"We can try that." She pulled away just far enough to allow their eyes to meet.

"And in the meantime, why don't you fill me in on what I missed of your movie while I shut down my laptop, and then I'll join you for the rest of it."

The brief could wait until tomorrow, while she was at work. It had only been an excuse, anyway.

"Okay," she said, finally sounding more at ease.

A few minutes later they were settled on the sofa, Brenna's upper body draped across his shoulder and chest. After shifting her to a better angle, he gently brushed her dark hair aside.

The pale triangle of skin exposed at her nape was too tempting to resist. She shivered as his lips grazed the spot. Then, tentatively, he slid his fingers up through her hair. He might not be a trained masseur, but he did have strong hands. Surely even a nonprofessional head rub would be welcome.

"Ahhhh." Her sigh of appreciation lodged somewhere in the vicinity of his chest.

He'd been shortchanging her. And she'd noticed and delicately called him on it.

His fingers kept moving, slowly circling, trying to mimic what he remembered feeling when Brenna had done this for him. The air conditioner droned in the background as she snuggled more deeply against him.

He could do better at getting to know her, as a person and not just as a bed partner. He *would* do better. She deserved at least that much.

Failure, he was gradually realizing, was not an option.

THE NUMBERS DIDN'T LIE. And they were telling Brenna that if something didn't change soon, Serenity Massage wouldn't even make it through the following spring. Just in time to have to explain her colossal failure to a bunch of judgmental classmates at her tenth college reunion. If she even bothered to go.

Her face felt hot just thinking about it. If she'd had a dying tech start-up instead of a massage therapy business, her classmates would commiserate with her over their Bombay-and-tonics and probably try to network her into a new situation. *Better luck next time. I'm sure you learned a lot from it.*

Instead, she knew exactly what they would be thinking. The same thing Gregory had said with a derisive bark of laughter when he'd dumped her no-longer-high-powered ass. Or the variation proffered by her mentor—well, her former mentor—at McKinsey, when she'd burst into his office and told him about the radical career change she wanted to make. *Why on earth would you throw away your degree on* that?

Why was it so hard to understand that not everyone defined success the same way?

Failure wasn't a foregone conclusion, though, at least not yet. There were a couple of things she could do to keep

Serenity Massage on life support a little longer. Because she knew precisely how her budget had gotten so unbalanced in the past month and a half. It was Cal. Or rather, keeping up with him when he came to visit.

Brenna knew it wasn't realistic, but she wanted to contribute more or less equally to their relationship. Being a kept woman wasn't her style. Cal was already flying up to Boston every weekend, bringing home expensive ingredients for the meals he sometimes cooked her, and taking her out for the occasional lunch or dinner. Buying luxuries like fresh strawberries or fluffy bagels and cream cheese and keeping a welcoming six-pack of some obscure microbrew in the fridge seemed the least she could do.

That wasn't the only way she'd been jeopardizing her financial solvency, though. No, she was also slowly killing her business on the revenue side of the equation. She'd been heedlessly cutting back her hours on weekends so she could spend more time with him. Just an appointment or two, here and there. But taken together, they'd added up.

The situation wasn't sustainable. Brenna knew that. It was just hard to want to do anything about it when she was already falling for him.

She'd confessed she'd gone to Stanford and worked at McKinsey because they needed to go beyond the superficial if they were ever going to be more than friends-with-benefits. And she didn't want to turn it into an even bigger deal by waiting longer to tell him. Besides, if he'd been a jerk about it, she would have her excuse to call things off and focus on reviving her business.

But their relationship had begun to shift after that fraught conversation. On Monday, he'd texted her, just to say hello. On Tuesday, he'd texted her again, which made her smile—Monday hadn't been a fluke. On Wednesday, *she'd* texted *him*. Their back-and-forth was still mostly of the "how's your day going" variety, but it showed he was thinking about her when they weren't together.

At first, she attributed his newfound interest to her academic and career pedigree—that she was now somehow qualified to be more than just his acquaintance-with-benefits. But that unflattering assessment soon gave way to something like hope. Because late Thursday night, after they were each at home and done with their workdays, he called her. And it wasn't just to make plans for Friday.

After chatting with her for a while, out of the blue he asked, "Why did you give up management consulting to become a massage therapist?"

He sounded sincerely interested, which made it easier to explain it to him than she'd expected. Though the fact that she could always end the conversation if he reacted negatively also helped.

"Look," she said. "My parents run a small business, and I went to Stanford on a scholarship and serious financial aid. Most of the time, I never really felt like I fit in there. There was a lot of pressure to follow the typical rat-race post-grad path, and Gregory, my boyfriend at the time, encouraged me toward management consulting. The stability of it made sense to me, because I've lived through the ups and downs of my parents' business. But it was a terrible fit. Even worse than Stanford."

"I'm sorry you had such a rough time in college. I

loved it at Stanford."

"And you love being at your law firm, too. I can tell. You're lucky."

He bristled a little, misinterpreting her. "What do you mean, lucky? I worked my ass off—"

"I know that. That's not what I meant." She tried to smooth his ruffled feathers. "I mean, you're lucky you've always known what you wanted to do, and you've been able to do it. You found something you're passionate about, you're really good at it, it pays you well, and the people who matter to you think it's prestigious."

It was a few moments before she could bring herself to continue. "Management consulting wasn't like that for me. It paid well and was prestigious, and I was good at it, but not good enough to ever become a director. Or want to. Because I wasn't passionate about it. Not the way my friend Cissy is. Sometimes I downright hated it," she admitted.

"What did you hate about it?"

"I had no ownership of my life. I was on the road most of the time, advising companies how to be more efficient, and that usually meant people losing their jobs. Sometimes hundreds of them at a time. It was sucking me dry."

It had been five years since she'd quit McKinsey to help others cope with their stressful lives, but some of the memories still left her throat achingly tight. Her next words sounded rough and small. "I didn't leave management consulting for massage therapy so other people would respect me. I left so I could respect myself."

Cal was quiet for a moment. "I guess I can understand that. And maybe I'm biased, but I think you're a fantastic massage therapist."

She exhaled silently, relieved, and dashed away the moisture that had formed in the corners of her eyes. "Thanks. It means a lot to me that you get it." Though deciding whether to end her friends-with-benefits experiment would have been so much easier if he hadn't.

He changed the subject then, and they talked for another ten or fifteen minutes about lighter topics before saying good night.

Before this past weekend, continuing to see Cal had seemed less and less worthwhile. She'd known it would only lead to heartache and Serenity Massage's even speedier demise. Now she had to find a way to fit a fledgling relationship with him into her life—and her budget.

There wasn't a lot of room to expand her hours during the week, but she supposed she could extend her evening hours out to ten o'clock. More importantly, she would just have to be more disciplined about accepting appointments during the weekends, even if it meant less time with Cal.

And if that didn't work, she could always ditch her energy bar habit. Eating regularly was overrated anyway.

10

CAL'S THURSDAY PHONE CALL with Brenna started out innocently enough. The sultry August night put both of them in mind of summers gone by.

He sat in the faux-suede armchair in his air-conditioned living room and told her about Julys and Augusts paper-pushing at his dad's law firm—which he'd actually enjoyed—and relaxing weekends at his parents' lake house. It was sometimes hard to go back to the lake house, now that his dad was gone.

Brenna had also spent her summers helping her parents with their business, custom-building traditional Japanese teahouses and designing Japanese gardens. She'd dug up yards and planted saplings, banged in the odd nail or two, helped with the books, "gofered" for the crews once she'd gotten her driver's license, and babysat her twin sisters. He saw her entrepreneurial spirit in a new light after he heard about all the hands-on experience she'd had growing up. She really was amazing.

And now he had to tell his amazing girlfriend—he couldn't deny that's what she was, at this point—that he had a work event tomorrow night that would keep him in DC until Saturday morning. One of the partners had asked him to step in at the last minute, and he couldn't turn down the opportunity—even though he knew he'd be struggling to keep the scowl off his face when he was supposed to be schmoozing with the clients. Brenna had gotten him good and hooked on her, and he didn't take kindly to anything that delayed his gratification, even by twelve hours.

"Aww." Her disappointment at his news sounded at least halfway sincere. "And I had all these plans for you."

"Were they…naked plans, by any chance?" he teased.

"Oh, yeah. Definitely."

He grinned. "Care to fill me in on any of these naked plans you had?"

"Hmm, let's see."

He didn't really expect her to take him up on the request. After all, they'd never had phone sex before. Flirted heavily, sure. But full-on, all-out dirty talking? She seemed too sweet to be into that.

Never in his life had he been more thrilled to be wrong.

"Well," she said saucily, "the first thing I wanted to do was strip off all your clothes, lay you down on my bed, and take your beautiful cock into my hot mouth. I don't think I've done that often enough, do you?"

A choked-off moan escaped Cal's lips. She hadn't really just said that, had she? His rapidly stiffening dick seemed to think so, but his brain couldn't keep up with the shocking direction their conversation had taken.

"Sounds like you agree." He could hear her dark smile.

"Holy shit, Bren, are you kidding me?" he sputtered.

"Hey, you asked."

It was true, he *had* asked. And now he was wishing he'd asked weeks ago.

He didn't realize he'd been waiting for her to continue until she said, "I'm touching myself, you know. My nipples are already hard." She was trying to sound nonchalant, but arousal thickened her words.

"Ohhh, that's hot." His erection twitched, hardening further in a surge of want. His breathing grew shallow as he listened intently for whatever she said next.

"Are you stroking yourself?"

"Not quite yet." He cupped a palm over the iron bar that was now tenting his athletic shorts. Anything more and he was afraid he'd go off like a rocket.

"Well, I've flipped up my skirt and I'm sliding my hand inside my panties, imagining it's you."

She wasn't playing fair. Cal was thirty-six hours and four hundred miles away from burying his raging hard-on inside her welcoming body, and everything she said merely intensified his craving for her.

Rasping out a curse, he tugged down the front of his shorts and boxers, setting himself mercifully free. A rapidly thinning strand stretched from his crown to the matching wet spot on the front of his boxers. He captured the slick thread between his thumb and fingertip.

"So much pre-come already. I'd slip into you so easy right now."

She gasped. "I want that so bad, Cal. I swear I'm dying for you."

With his thumb riding on top of his shaft and two slick fingers underneath it, he began a slow, easy glide. Carefully, torturously slow. "Yessss," he hissed out. "Tell me more about that hot mouth of yours."

"Yeah? I'd take you as deep as I could. It would feel so hot, so wet inside my mouth. And then I'd lick my way up your shaft until just the very tip of you was still inside my lips. Mmm," she hummed, and he could imagine the gentle vibration against that most sensitive area.

He pulled up his T-shirt, because he knew where this was headed. Then he fisted his cock, his caressing motion shading into a firmer grip and faster tempo. "Oh, God. That sounds about a million times better than how I'll actually be spending my Friday night."

"That's just the beginning. Then I'd kiss my way up across your hipbone, your belly, your chest…definitely your nipples." The rhythmic strain in her voice as she sped up her efforts was delicious.

With a groan, he started working himself faster, too.

"I'd straddle your hips and thighs—God, your thighs, you'd be tensing them up and I just want to dig my fingertips into those gorgeous muscles—and I'd get you all lined up with me, so we'd both know that one stroke would have you all the way inside me." She paused to draw in a shaky breath. "You wouldn't believe how wet I am right now."

"Ah, Bren." His voice was tight, his control starting to unravel. "Don't do that to me. I don't want to come before you do." But the soft gasp she responded with only ramped up his arousal.

"Tell me how you'd make me come," she demanded.

"I hope you're in the mood to be fucked hard. Because if I were there right now, I don't think I'd be able to stop myself."

"Yeah, I need it just like that."

He grunted. "I'd grab your hips and pull you down onto my cock, so fucking deep. Ah, Christ."

"I'm getting close," she warned him.

Cal's breathing grew harsher, his pace more frantic. Not long now. "Tell me what you're doing."

"Mmm, I'm rubbing my clit with the side of my hand, and I've got two fingers inside me. Feels so good," she panted.

"Ohhh, you are so fuckin' hot, Bren." It was a struggle to hold himself back. "I love listening to you talk dirty to me. I'm jerkin' my cock real hard. Come with me, babe. I want to hear you."

She whimpered, and a bolt of lust drove right through him. A sudden rush of pleasure sent him past the point of no return. "Ah, Jesus. Fuck, I'm coming!"

His hips pressed up into his greedy fist, and the first spurt burst from his shaft, splattering his chest. With a drawn-out groan, he striped his belly with a second spurt, then a third and a fourth.

He fell back against the chair, panting hard. "Come for me," he urged her, his voice shredded.

"I'm right there." Her words were taut with tension. "Ooh, yes!" she squealed, and he wanted more than anything to have her pressed right up against him then, body to body, sweaty and gasping and shattering into pieces around him.

"So good," she sighed, trailing off into a silence broken only by their ragged breathing.

A few moments later she said his name, a hoarse, trembling question.

It was a miracle he was able to answer in a steady voice, because his stomach muscles were still twitching, and his heart was pounding like he'd just finished a stadium run. "What, babe?"

"I miss you," she said, her voice a soft caress.

He paused, then replied, "I miss you, too."

"Mmm," she cooed, which turned into a yawn. "Gosh, sorry." She chuckled. "Long day just caught up to me."

"Yeah, I know how that is." Lord, did he know how that was. But he was reluctant to end their call, even though Brenna was clearly exhausted. "Get some rest then," he said, wishing he were there to tuck her in.

"Okay. I'll see you Saturday morning." She yawned again. "Good night, Cal."

"Night, Bren."

He hung up, frowning as he scanned the room for a nearby box of tissues. Brenna had seemed more tired than usual lately, and she'd been getting home later, too. He hadn't forgotten that seemingly offhand remark a few weeks ago about her difficult financial situation. Longer hours must be her answer.

Cal was accustomed to long workdays, and he supposed Brenna must be too, given her former life as a management consultant. He just wished he could do more than distract her from the stress she must be under. She would probably resist any offer of financial help though, and it seemed too soon to make one, anyway.

What could he do to ease her burdens this weekend? Pack her some healthy lunches, to make sure she ate during the day. Cook her dinner, or maybe take her out. Definitely make her come, as many times as possible.

That last thought had him smiling. Brenna wasn't the only one who could make naked plans.

AT THE END OF THEIR BEST weekend yet, Brenna twined her arms around Cal's neck, tugging him down for yet another languorous good-bye kiss. His tongue thrust masterfully into her mouth, his lips a soft, slick pressure against her own. Then, when she returned the favor, his gentle suction against her tongue nearly buckled her knees.

Christ, Cal was a phenomenal kisser. And she wanted him. Again.

She began a slow grind against him, an almost imperceptible roll of her hips. He groaned in response.

"Can't get enough of you, Bren," he gasped as he wove his hands into her hair. His lips came down on hers again, more urgently this time.

Of course, she kissed him back. How could she not? But when they came up for air, she put her hands on his chest, saying, "Don't start what you can't finish." Then she smiled ruefully. "We'd better stop. I don't want to send you off with a boner."

"Too late." Cal repositioned himself inside his cargo shorts, a maneuver not even he could make look graceful.

But he wiped the grin right off her face when his hands curved around her hips and he snugged her right up against his hard, hot ridge. "Maybe we *shouldn't* stop, so you *don't* send me off with a boner."

Her smile was back, even as she protested, "There isn't time. Don't you only have, like, ten minutes before you need to get a cab?"

"I could accomplish a lot in ten minutes…"

Her concern that he'd miss his flight won out over her desire to make quite sure he did. Brenna extricated herself from his embrace. "Come over here." She led him to the living room before flouncing onto the sofa. "In the absence of a chaperone, you'll have to sit there for our chat." The picture of primness, she motioned him to the armchair.

Cal raised an eyebrow, though he sank into the chair without too much protest. "What, I can't even sit next to you?"

She shook her head. "Too volatile. I can pretty much guarantee you'd miss your flight if you did that." She suggestively eyed the erection tenting his shorts. "We can always pick it back up next weekend. Can't we?"

"Ye—es." He extended the word like a pouty twelve-year-old.

She would have laughed, but her girly parts wholeheartedly agreed with him.

Brenna firmly ignored said girly parts. "Hey, that reminds me. You're coming up for Labor Day weekend, right? Cissy's moving in with her boyfriend, and they're having a housewarming barbecue thing."

Her stomach flipped as she considered her next words, but after the fantastic weekend she and Cal had just had, she steeled herself and said them anyway. "I'd like you to get to know some of my friends. I know you've seen Mel and Rikki around the building, but Cissy's my best friend, and this would be a great chance to spend a little time with her."

She had kind of been taking for granted they'd see each other over the holiday weekend, just like every other weekend since they'd gotten together. So his answer dashed a cold bucket of reality over her, shocking her into silence.

"Uh, probably not, actually." At least he had the grace to look sheepish. "One of my friends is getting married that weekend."

It felt like an eternity before she could speak. "Okay." She was unable to keep the skepticism and hurt from tingeing her drawn-out syllables.

It wasn't so much that he hadn't asked her to attend this wedding with him, though that did sting a little. They had only recently begun to grow closer, and he might have accepted the wedding invitation months ago. Or maybe it was someplace far away and he'd already bought his ticket to get there. There was a whole host of perfectly acceptable reasons he might not have asked her to come with him.

What was more upsetting was that Labor Day was only three weekends from now, and he'd surely *known* he was going to this wedding for a while. It was just so damned…inconsiderate, is what it was. He had to have realized she would want to spend the long weekend with him—and if that wasn't going to happen, then she would want time to make alternate plans. When had he planned on telling her he wasn't coming up? Two days before?

She was about to ask him that very question when the silence apparently became too much for him. He would have been better off apologizing, or even saying nothing at all. Instead, every word that came out of his mouth just made it worse.

"Bren, don't be like that." Cal's brows drew together in annoyance.

"Like what?"

"If you're pissed off with me, we should talk about it."

"There's nothing to talk about."

"Look." He exhaled in frustration. "I didn't want to ask you to come with me because I know you don't have the money or time, and I didn't want to offer to pay to fly you down because it would've felt…awkward. And there are going to be a lot of people I know from work there, and I didn't want to tell anyone about us while I'm still up for partner."

She'd been more or less with him until that stunner right at the end. "Are you—you're not embarrassed by me, are you?"

He looked stricken. But he hesitated before saying, "No, of course not. Why would I be embarrassed by you?"

Cal was such a horrible liar.

"You *are*," she said softly, incredulously.

The brutal silence continued until she broke it with a single word, her voice low with disappointment and vibrating with anger.

"Coward."

"Brenna!" he protested.

She stood abruptly. "You need to go. We're done."

Cal stood as well and took a step toward her. "Wait! We can't be done. Please don't just give up on us like this. I—you know you mean a lot to me." His voice actually sounded ragged around the edges, like he was overcome with emotions he'd barely expressed to her. "Please. Just…give me a chance to work it out with you." He paused before continuing in a lower voice, as if the admission pained him. "I need you."

"What for? To be your fuck-buddy? I thought we'd moved beyond that, but I guess I was wrong." She flung the words at him, and he winced. Her laughter sounded hollow to her own ears. "The sex may be good, but I told you before, that's not enough for me."

Of course, he completely missed her point. "What do you mean, *good*? The sex is amazing, and you know it!"

"Okay, you win, Mr. Lawyer. It's amazing. You've raised the bar. Happy?"

"I haven't raised the bar, I *broke* the damn bar."

"You know what? You're probably right. But it doesn't matter, because I need more than that. I *deserve* more than that. I need to be with someone who supports my choice of career and is proud of what I do. I need someone who might be able to...love me back."

Cal just stared at her, stunned.

She pressed her trembling lips together. There was no way in hell she was going to cry in front of him. "You need to go," she repeated. "You're going to miss your flight."

He swore and closed the remaining distance between them. "We're *not* done. Not until we talk about it. I'll call you tomorrow morning."

Her chin went up. "Don't bother. I won't answer."

"Brenna, how can I fix this if you won't talk to me?"

"You can't." She tried to sound strong, confident, convincing, but the shakiness she despised had already crept into her voice. She needed him to leave, *now*. Before the tears started. So she said the words necessary to accomplish that. "I've realized this isn't going to work for me anymore, and you need to accept that."

He searched her face, and she took the opportunity for one last look at him. So she saw the exact second he gave in, his shoulders slumping into a dejected posture.

His voice was hoarse as he entreated her. "Can I—can I kiss you one more time? Before I go?"

The bitter taste of disappointment overwhelmed her. She knew she'd be angry with him later, but right now, she needed one last kiss more than she needed to breathe.

If she said anything, she'd start crying, so she simply nodded her assent.

As his lips descended on hers, a lump rose in her throat. His kiss started out sweet, so achingly sweet, a tender brushing of lips. And then his arms enfolded her, warm and strong, his scent surrounding her. It just felt so damn *good,* being pressed against him. Her arms came up, too, and she gripped the back of his shirt, clinging to him for these last few moments, not wanting to let him go, even though she knew she'd never really had him in the first place.

So this is what good-bye feels like.

She broke away from him then, on an indrawn breath that sounded nearly like a sob.

"I'll miss you," he said. A suspicious shimmer turned his eyes to molten silver.

"I'm sure you'll get over me." Her voice was rough, her throat aching so fiercely she could barely get the words out.

His next words were so softly spoken, she wasn't sure he'd meant her to hear them at all. "I'm not."

He strode the few paces to the foyer and bent down to

grab his bags. Then he straightened once more. With a harsh sigh, he opened the door. Half-turning to look back at her, he said, "I'm sorry."

And then he walked away, allowing the door to close behind him, and the tears she'd been holding back scalded her cheeks as they began to fall, one by one.

11

IT HAD BEEN SEVENTY-TWO HOURS since Brenna unceremoniously dumped him, and Cal was still bewildered. Not to mention pissed off and moping, and sometimes all three.

He'd worked his ass off since he'd gotten back to DC, as usual. But he missed her. His muscles ached, and his normally boundless energy had deserted him. It felt like the flu, but he knew better. It was her. Her absence had created a craving that could never be assuaged.

So he kept billing the hours during the day like a good little worker bee, and late at night, once the summer heat died down, he went on five-mile runs, blasting his "Fuck the World" playlist.

He hadn't noticed it before, but he'd gotten used to winding down his day on the phone with Brenna, or exchanging text messages when she had a break between appointments. He didn't even want to think about how shitty he'd feel on Friday, when he should have been flying up to see her. Instead he'd be spending his first weekend in months without her.

He revisited their argument again and again, considering what he could have said or done Sunday night to generate a different outcome. Not opening his big fat mouth in the first place, for one thing.

And how many times had Brenna reiterated the importance of her business and her career? Yet when she'd asked if he was embarrassed by her, he'd frozen. Stupid, stupid, idiot.

Then there was that other thing she'd said. The thing that had completely floored him, though it shouldn't have been a surprise, because his own feelings had been inexorably moving in the same direction. Which made his deer-in-the-headlights act when she'd obliquely mentioned the L-word his crowning achievement in that evening's unadulterated stupidity.

"Wilcox. Snap out of it."

His head jerked toward the door. Jordan Castle, a junior partner who was also Cal's closest friend at the firm, regarded him with arms crossed, a forbidding expression on his face.

"What happened to knocking, so you can politely announce your presence?"

Uninvited, Jordie stalked into Cal's office and closed the door behind him. "Can that shit, Wilcox."

He bristled. "What's your problem?"

Jordie shook his head, tight-lipped. "Got back this afternoon from taking depositions in Chicago. I heard you've been closeted in your office all this week. People are starting to talk."

Cal's heart sank into his stomach. *Shit.* But he tried to play it cool. "About what?"

"Some people think maybe you're job hunting. But you're not doing that, are you? Because that would piss me off. I backed you for partner, and you never once said anything—"

"I'm not," Cal said in a low voice.

Jordie appraised him for a moment, then the tension drained out of his stance. "Yeah, you look too shattered for that. What's up?"

"I don't want to talk about it."

His friend's eyes narrowed. "It's a girl, isn't it," he surmised, not even bothering to make it a question.

And there was the reason Jordie had been named a Rising Star litigator last year. Too damned perceptive.

"So, tell me how you fucked up."

Cal enunciated more clearly. "I said, I'm not talking about it with you."

Instead of taking the hint, Jordie pulled out one of Cal's guest chairs and sat down, steepling his fingers. "Fine. Maybe this will cheer you up." From the way Jordie's brown eyes were dancing behind his frameless glasses, he apparently had some good news to share.

Sighing, Cal turned back to his computer. "At least let me sign out of my search." As he'd learned early in his career, clients got really ticked off if you left the meter running on your Westlaw searches while chatting with someone.

"So," Jordie said, "you should make sure you block off the first weekend in November on your calendar."

Cal frowned. That wasn't at all what he'd expected to hear. He brought up his schedule, saying over his shoulder, "Why, you planning to elope that weekend or something?"

"Nope. I'll be in New York City for the Partner Prom, with the rest of the partners."

The Partner Prom, despite its ridiculous name, was actually a pretty swanky event from everything Cal had heard. All the partners in CMH's US offices were invited to bring their significant other to a delicious catered dinner, followed by cocktails and dancing, where everyone wore formal attire and got impressively sloshed. Those from out of town were flown in and put up overnight at a high-end hotel.

And then Cal froze, hands hovering over the keyboard, as it all clicked into place. "No," he breathed as he turned back to his friend, his heartbeat speeding up. The man's grin was bigger than he'd ever seen it. "Really?"

Jordie nodded. "But you can't tell a *soul* before the official announcement. I mean it. Not your mom, not your secretary, not your best friend from college. *No one.*"

The ache in his chest leveled him yet again. The three people he most wanted to share this secret with were Brenna, and his parents. And two of them were no longer in his life. His shoulders sagged, but he tried to sound excited for Jordie's benefit. "No problem. That's awesome," he said, forcing his lips into a smile.

Jordie shook his head. "I can tell your heart's not in it, and that's not good, because this is a big deal. Tell me about her. Maybe it'll make you feel better."

Cal doubted it. "She's up in Boston. I started seeing her in May, but in the past few weeks things had been getting more serious."

"Why is this the first time I'm hearing about her, then?"

Cal shrugged. Keeping his relationship secret had been another tactical error he'd be more than happy to

rectify if Brenna ever forgave him. And if the partners—
no, wait, the *other* partners—didn't like it, so be it. Despite
his mindset in recent weeks, CMH wasn't the only law
firm out there. Besides, a lateral move to another firm—if
CMH forced his hand—would be easier as a partner than
a senior associate.

"Wait, Boston—what, did you meet her when you
were up there for that trial?" The man may as well have
been a mind reader.

"Well…" Cal trailed off, unwilling to describe the circumstances under which he'd gotten together with
Brenna.

Jordie took his lack of elaboration as a yes. "Dude, I'm
impressed. How on earth did you manage to hook up with
someone while you were at trial? I barely have time to eat
and sleep."

"We didn't get together until after the trial was over.
And that's all I'm going to say about it."

"What did you say she did?"

He hadn't, of course—but that had never stopped
Jordie from fishing for info before. "She's, um, a massage
therapist," Cal said.

Jordie laughed. "Ah, so that's how you met her."

Cal actually felt the heat rushing into his cheeks as he
exercised his right to remain silent, confirmation enough
for Jordie.

"I can't believe you were dating a massage therapist
for three months, and you never said a word."

"Yeah, what of it?"

Jordie raised his hands in the universal *settle down*
gesture. "Hey, take it easy. You know I wouldn't have

judged. Not that I can speak for everyone at the firm."

"That's exactly why I never said anything about it. And now we stopped seeing each other anyway, so there would have been no point." Or maybe that was the point. Who knew anymore?

"You want my advice?"

"That would be a no."

Leaning forward, Jordie ignored him. "Get her a present. Something that shows her how much you care about her."

Cal scowled. Though it wasn't a bad idea, actually.

"It's obvious you do care about her. I've never seen you this torqued up over a woman, not the entire time I've known you."

"Thank you, Dr. Phil." Cal capped his sarcasm with the classic lawyer brush-off. "I'll take it under advisement."

"Fine. Ignore my words of wisdom. Just trying to help."

"I know. And I appreciate it." Then he smiled for the first time since he'd left Brenna's apartment. Because in that instant, at last, he came up with a plan. "But I think I've got this."

"All right." Jordie stood. "Well, have at it, then. At least you don't look like someone kicked your puppy anymore."

"Way to boost a guy's confidence."

Jordie grinned. "My work here is done. And I expect an introduction to your golden unicorn at the Partner Prom."

Before Cal could ask what a golden unicorn was, Jordie's eyes lit up. "We should bill this point-one to the new mentoring program."

That got the first laugh out of Cal in days. Though he supposed the past six minutes did qualify as mentoring, in a way. "I'll do it if you do it."

"Deal," Jordie agreed.

"Thanks for letting me know about…that information, by the way."

"Absolutely. No way I wanted you to hear it from someone else. Anyway, wanna call it a night and grab a beer before you head home?"

It beat the hell out of drinking alone. "Sure. Why not."

Jordie stood. "I'll stop by and grab you in about fifteen minutes. We'll hit Cleary's." Then he lowered his voice and held out his hand. "Congrats, man. You deserve it."

"Thanks." Cal clapped his hand into Jordie's for a shake. "See you in a bit."

First, he had some presents to buy.

"WHAT'S THIS?" BRENNA ASKED MARCUS, the UPS guy. It was a silly question, because he couldn't know what was in the medium-sized cardboard box any more than she could.

Predictably, Marcus shrugged. "Beats me." He hefted it a couple of times as she provided her electronic signature for the package. "Doesn't weigh that much. Four, five pounds, maybe."

The unexpected delivery on Friday morning was a bright spot in what had otherwise been a pretty rough week. She should have been angry with Cal for the lack of respect he'd shown for her time and choice of profession—and she was—but she'd been gripped predominantly by disappointment and grief since their breakup. He'd been so close to perfect in so many ways, and just when she'd thought their relationship might actually be moving beyond the friends-with-benefits arrangement that had never sat well with her, he'd tumbled right off her pedestal.

His spectacular failings didn't stop her body from remembering all the incredible things he knew how to do to her, though. Or all the pleasure he'd brought her. And they didn't stop her heart from aching, either.

Brenna forced the depressing thoughts from her mind and exchanged Marcus's tablet for her package, thanking him. After seeing him out, she examined the box more closely. There were no clues to the sender's identity. She would just have to open it.

Two dozen individually wrapped dried fruit and nut bars nestled amongst environmentally sound crinkled paper strips. A brochure proclaimed the "High Energy Snack Bars" to be from the White Pine Bakery in Burlington, Vermont. They looked delicious, and much healthier than the energy bars she used to buy. One end of each bar was dipped in chocolate—artisanal, small-batch chocolate from sustainable rainforest sources, according to the brochure.

But who were they from? She had a suspicion, but was holding out unrealistic hope her mother had sent a care package. For the first time since college.

Digging around in the box, Brenna finally found what she was seeking. A small, square envelope contained a card, which read: *I miss you. And I knew this was the only way*

I could be sure you'd eat.

Infuriatingly, the energy bars looked too yummy for Brenna and her growling stomach to refuse them. And no matter how she felt about Cal, she couldn't accept his gift without acknowledging it.

So she texted him: *Thanks for the energy bars.*

He responded almost immediately. *They aren't energy bars. They're highly nutritious snacks, lovingly handmade in the woods of Vermont from the freshest of ingredients.*

Her eyes narrowed, and she picked up the brochure again. There were his words, stolen straight from the marketing copy.

She smiled wryly. He knew how to amuse her, but a box of glorified candy bars and some sentimental words weren't going to be nearly enough to make up for what he'd said. Not after his revelation last weekend that he was too ashamed of her profession to want to introduce her to his work colleagues.

Another text notification warbled, interrupting her thoughts. *Did you eat lunch today?*

It was almost three o'clock. No wonder her stomach was feeling so empty. Not that she'd had much of an appetite, lately. *No comment*, she responded.

Please eat. I still worry about you.

Her mood shifted abruptly from annoyance to desolation, and she squeezed her eyes shut, trying to keep upwelling tears from spilling over. Another client was due shortly, and Brenna couldn't look like the mess she was inside.

I need to go. Thanks again. She ended their conversation, shutting off her phone before he could entice her into lingering, and before she began to cry in earnest.

Sighing, she unwrapped one of the gourmet snack bars and took a bite from the chocolate-dipped end. It undoubtedly would have tasted much better if she hadn't had to force it down past the lump in her throat.

For the entire next week she struggled to forget about Cal, his caring words haunting her every time she raided the box of energy bars. He didn't try to communicate with her again, which ought to have made it easier to pretend he hadn't broken her heart. But with Cissy texting and calling her on a daily basis to check in and provide support, his betrayal was, paradoxically, harder to get over.

By the time Friday rolled around again, she still hadn't heard a thing from him. She was regretting that she'd agreed to meet Cissy at Ciro's for a quick lunch, because there was a distinct possibility she would end up crying in public. And besides, she'd have to lock up Serenity Massage while she was out, and what if Cal sent her a present when she wasn't there to receive it?

On the plus side, the Canadian bacon, pineapple, and egg pizza she and Cissy ended up sharing was almost divine enough to take her mind off her troubles. At least until midway through their second slices, when Cissy asked how she was doing.

"I'm fine," Brenna said.

Cissy regarded her with sympathy and worry. "You don't look fine. You look like you haven't been taking care of yourself."

"Okay. I *will* be fine, then."

Cissy just kept looking at her, a concerned frown wrinkling her forehead.

Brenna sighed. "Honestly?" Cissy nodded her encouragement, and Brenna leaned across the table so she didn't have to shout her misery to the restaurant at large. "So he gave me the energy bars last Friday, and we texted. And since then—nothing. I'm annoyed with myself that that bothers me, because I'm the one that broke up with him. But I still can't stop wondering if he's thinking of me as often as I've been thinking of him."

"Oh, Bren." Cissy's eyes were shining now, in her empathetic distress. "I'm so sorry."

"It's okay. I meant it when I said I'll be fine. I needed to focus harder on saving Serenity Massage, anyway. He was a huge distraction."

"He was a lot of things." From her gentle tone, Cissy meant the good kind of things.

And that's all it took for Brenna to get choked up. Again.

She dropped the rest of her pizza slice back onto her plate. "I can't eat the rest of this."

Now Cissy looked horrified, probably feeling guilty that she'd instigated the conversation. "Bren... You have to eat," she said.

"It's not that bad. I'll have them pack up the rest of the pizza to go. And if I get hungry, I've still got the rest of the energy bars." They both smiled weakly at Brenna's attempted joke, though Cissy still looked on the verge of tears, and Brenna's brave front felt pretty shaky.

Like the incomparably excellent friend she was, Cissy paid for their lunch and walked the two blocks back to Serenity Massage with Brenna. When they reached the front steps of her building, Cissy gave her a long hug that felt wonderful, but also reminded her once again of her loss. Then, before flagging down a cab, Cissy made Brenna promise to text her if she needed anything.

Her belly half-full and her heart half-empty, Brenna was straightening up the therapy rooms between early-afternoon clients when the doorbell chimed. Her heartbeat sped up as she hurried to the suite's glass door. A young man stood on the other side of it, wearing a light blue polo shirt with the logo of one of the fanciest florists in the city. He held another medium-sized cardboard box; this one was shaped like a cube.

The grin that spread across Brenna's face was unreasonably broad. And she couldn't seem to return her expression to normal, either.

She let the guy in. He set the box down on a side table with care and opened it while she signed for the delivery. Then he pulled out an exquisitely trimmed bonsai with pale pink flowers in an oval stoneware pot. She swallowed a sigh as she appreciated its perfection.

"Where would you like me to put this?" he asked.

"The table where you've got it is fine."

He straightened the bonsai in the center of the table before handing Brenna the card that had accompanied her new plant. She thanked him, and he picked up the now-empty cardboard box. Wishing her a good afternoon, he left.

Her hands trembling slightly, she opened the tiny envelope. This time, the message simply said: *I still miss you. Especially on Fridays.*

Brenna exhaled a shaky breath. She still missed Cal, too. Way too much.

She didn't have a lot of time before her next client arrived, so she snapped a quick picture of the bonsai and added a text message, thanking him for it.

As before, his response was almost immediate. *I'm so glad you like it. The flowers reminded me of the cherry blossoms around the Tidal Basin in April. They're spectacular.*

Well. That was very...neutral. She almost expected him to follow up with a play for the two of them to get back together, maybe a suggestion that he could show her the cherry blossoms next year, or something like that. But he seemed to be waiting for her to respond.

She should have gracefully exited their conversation and gotten back to prepping the room her one-thirty client had just vacated. But she was loath to cop out like she had after last Friday's gift.

So she responded with what she thought was another neutral observation. *Did you know that bonsai can live for hundreds of years?*

I did, he replied. *That's why I wanted to get one for you.*

The icy chill that had surrounded her heart for nearly two weeks began to thaw. Cal might be subtle about it, but he didn't mess around. He was definitely wooing her. And that realization was absurdly pleasing.

Maybe, just maybe, she'd be able to forgive him. *If* he could get past his issues with her being a massage therapist. Because choosing between her business and their relationship wasn't something she was willing to do. And neither was settling for being his secret girlfriend. She deserved better than that.

The doorbell chimed again—her next client was here. Out of time, she fired off a quick reply: *Sweet-talker.*

Her phone vibrated as she was setting it to silent. The incorrigible man had sent her a smiley face.

Cal was quiet for a few days after that, but this time she didn't have to wait until Friday to hear from him. On Monday night he texted her, right around the time they used to talk on the phone. But with her last appointment of the day over at eight o'clock, she went to bed early and didn't see his *Hey* until the next morning. She decided not to respond, but her heart still did a giddy little dance because he'd been thinking of her.

He tried again Tuesday night. This time she was awake and on alert, her phone nearby, just in case.

Hi, she responded.

How was your day?

Pretty good. Long. How about you?

Day was okay. Also long. Just came back from a run.

He ran? She supposed he could have been running during those Saturdays and Sundays he'd been visiting her, while she'd been at work. He sure as hell didn't get that body by sitting behind a desk all day.

And now she needed to stop thinking about Cal's beautifully muscled body, or this conversation would go sideways before she knew it.

Her phone warbled with the arrival of another message. *How's business?*

She appreciated that he'd asked, and not just because she could talk about Serenity Massage without the risk of wayward thoughts. *Better than usual lately. If it keeps up I might cut back my schedule again soon.*

Glad things are going well.

Brenna was trying to think of something else to say,

or to ask, when his next message came through.

Hate to cut this short, but I still need a shower.

Okay. Good night. Aaand back to thinking about his body again.

Wednesday and Thursday nights were more of the same, and then it was Friday again, with Labor Day weekend looming on the horizon. Feeling daring, she texted him late that morning. And waited. And saw three clients, back-to-back. And then waited some more.

It was hard not to revert to foolish high-school fears of having driven Cal off, having said the wrong thing, having proven too easy to catch. Even though it would be hard to go wrong with *Hi.* But the day wore on, and he sent neither word nor one of the presents she'd already grown accustomed to receiving. She wished she hadn't let him get her expectations up.

At around five o'clock, her phone finally buzzed, and her heart lurched with relief when she checked the screen.

Sorry I missed your text earlier! Unexpectedly had to attend a hearing today. Down in Florida. It's about a million degrees, I think I'm melting.

Brenna immediately pictured Cal in his suit pants and dress shirt—tie and jacket already removed—with his shirtsleeves rolled up to reveal those gorgeous, lightly tanned forearms she'd admired since day one. Now she was the one who was melting.

Hope it went well, she responded.

Well enough, he texted back. *Headed to airport now. Sorry today's present is going to be lame.*

Ooh, there was still going to be a present!

A picture came through of the snake plant she'd given

him, thriving away in his living room. He'd brought it home, and he'd cared for it this whole time. Somehow, that was an even better present than anything tangible could have been.

The picture also represented a glimpse into his life in DC, where he'd never previously invited her. She zoomed in on the rest of the image, hungrily searching for the details of how he lived. The dark wood furniture with neutral beige upholstery and the sleek chrome reading lamp in the background gave her an impression of modernity and solid masculinity. Thank God, no messy or tacky bachelor pad for Cal.

Then his accompanying message arrived. *You were right—it IS tough to kill. I'm glad I have something green in my apartment. And that you gave it to me.*

Ah, the wooing. The corners of Brenna's lips drifted upward.

Then he said: *Also a present for me today, much less lame.* And he texted her a link. When she clicked through, a press release from his law firm opened up, announcing and congratulating CMH's new partners. There was Calvin Wilcox, Jr., at the bottom of the list.

She couldn't help being thrilled for him. This was such a huge accomplishment, she was surprised he hadn't led off with the news. *OMG! Congrats! You must be so happy. You did it!*

It helps, he said, and she imagined his shrug. *Been kind of preoccupied lately.*

With?

You. Us.

And just like that, he laid it on the line, setting her

heart skittering crazily in her chest.

He didn't give her time to respond before he texted, *Gotta go, cab just pulled up at the airport, and I'm late for my flight. Miss you, Bren.*

"I miss you too," she said into the silence. Then she decided, what the hell, and texted it to him.

The fifteen minutes before he responded stretched to infinity. But the little blushing smiley face he finally sent made her day.

12

THE SWING BAND'S HORN SECTION blared from the ball-room, obnoxiously loud even from Cal's seat around the corner at the hotel bar. Forehead resting in his hands, he was already halfway to drunk, though he doubted he'd allow himself to get all the way there. Not considering how many wedding guests were also his work colleagues.

Someone approached from his right, and he looked up from his Bombay and tonic. Lara, a recently-made partner in one of CMH's specialty litigation practices, slid onto the seat next to him, setting her long, artfully tousled blonde hair swinging and displaying a tasteful hint of cleavage.

"How can you need cheering up? You just made partner! Come dance with me, you'll feel better."

Even half-lit, he couldn't mistake the sultry invitation in her voice. He cocked his head, weighing his options.

Outright rejection seemed rude, and would be awkward next time he saw her. Lara was sort of a friend, the kind he'd eat lunch with as part of a larger group every so often. And she was sort of pretty, if you were into blondes. Which he had been, before Brenna so thoroughly rocked his world.

Brenna. The reason he was self-medicating at the bar

rather than partying with Jordie and his other work friends. He'd truly been the worst kind of idiot. He should have asked her to come to the wedding with him. Then he would have been dancing with her, instead of getting hit on by someone he was completely uninterested in, whom he'd have to try to avoid in the office next week.

"Ummm," he finally said, buying some time before he had to just give Lara a flat-out no. He contemplated his drink, hoping for inspiration.

A miracle came in the form of Jordie, inserting himself halfway into the space between their seats. "Hey, Lara. Whatever you just asked him, Cal regretfully declines. He's been hung up on this girl in Boston for the past few weeks, so he's pretty much useless now."

Cal watched the comprehension dawn on Lara's face. "Dude," he protested weakly, shaking his head. "What the fuck?" He was definitely over being worried about the idea of his colleagues knowing about Brenna, but his continuing misery was none of their business.

Her expression turned to pity, which was even worse. "Aw, that's sweet." Then she shifted her attention to Jordie. Shrugging a tanned shoulder, she said, "I'd asked him to dance." She paused to look him up and down. "But you'll do nicely in a pinch."

Jordie smiled his charming, trial-winning smile. "How can I refuse an invitation like that? It's always been an ambition of mine to do nicely in a pinch."

Lara simpered—actually simpered. "Has it really?"

Jordie grinned. "No."

She pouted prettily at him.

Cal rolled his eyes so hard they ached. At least that

gave him a temporary respite from watching Jordie and Lara flirt with each other.

Too temporary by half, unfortunately.

Jordie grazed Lara's shoulder with exploratory finger-tips. Pitching his voice several tones lower, he said, "I'll dance with you anyway, though."

The urge to plug his ears and say "na-na-na-na" until it was over was almost irresistible. Instead, Cal swallowed the last few gulps of his drink, then shoved himself more or less upright. "Ugh. I'm outta here."

Jordie straightened too. "You all right?"

"Yeah. Just had enough."

His friend nodded. "Hey. Before you go, give me your phone."

"Huh?"

Jordie wore a dead-pan expression. "Trust me. You'll thank me in the morning." Then he leaned toward Cal again and stage-whispered, "No drunk-texting her, okay?"

Lara cracked up.

"Fine," Cal said, slapping his phone into Jordie's wait-ing palm. "Whatever. Just leave me in peace. And try not to wake me up when you come in."

Jordie turned toward him as Lara giggled in Cal's pe-ripheral vision. He leaned closer to Cal and said in his ear, "Not sure I'll be coming back to the room tonight. But if I do, I pwomise to be vewwy vewwy quiet."

Cal twitched involuntarily away from him, trying to escape the uncomfortable moment. "Jesus Christ, you guys. I need to leave five minutes ago, so I can unhear that."

Their laughter chased him across the echoing lobby as

he walked with exaggerated care back to his room.

Alone. Like he deserved.

Once settled in his room, the bed tempted him to lie down for just a few minutes, until he could drum up some motivation to get undressed and brush his teeth. But he knew from experience that never ended as planned. Besides, he wasn't *completely* drunk.

After taking off his shoes, he tugged his dark red silk tie out of its half Windsor knot and draped it across the desk chair. He dropped his dress shirt on top of the tie without ceremony, while his socks earned a place of honor on the floor. But he hung his light gray suit jacket and pants in the closet. They were linen, and he just couldn't bear to let them wrinkle in a careless pile overnight.

Wearing only his boxers, he brushed his teeth perfunctorily and downed a couple of Advil with a big glass of water. Like he had a prayer of staving off the hangover awaiting him tomorrow morning.

He lay on his bed, wondering what Brenna was doing. It was after eleven. Was she already asleep? Or maybe she was still at her friends' barbecue housewarming thing she'd invited him to. Knowing her, probably in bed already, he decided.

Wherever she was, he wished he were there, with her. There was nothing like the feeling of contentment that used to wash over him when they were whispering in the dark, her pert little butt snuggled against his front.

He rolled toward the bedside table, fully intending to switch off the lamp.

The red light on the room phone stared at him with

its unblinking eye.

Cal stared back at it.

He caved.

He had to hear her voice, and then he could sleep. Picking up the handset, he dialed Brenna's number from memory. Then he shut off the bedside lamp as he waited for her voice mail to pick up.

"Hello, this is Brenna."

He was too stunned to speak. She'd actually answered. She was trying to sound professional, but he knew that drowsy, late-night rasp. He'd woken her, but she hadn't been sleeping long.

"Hello?"

If he didn't say something soon, she would hang up on him. And he couldn't have that.

"Oh my God. Brenna. Your voice. It's so amazing to hear you." The words tumbled from his mouth haphazardly, each vying to express the hot rush of emotion surging through him.

"*Cal?*" Her tone was pure incredulity, but hearing his name from her lips after so many weeks still made him damn near euphoric.

"Yeah, sorry. Yeah. Hi."

"What number is this? Where are you? Are you okay?" Now she sounded alarmed.

He hastened to reassure her. "Yeah, I'm fine. Sorry. It's the hotel. That stupid wedding."

"Where's your phone?"

"I—Jordie made me give it to him."

"Who's Jordie? And why'd he make you give him your phone?" Finally, a smile lurked in her voice.

Relief flooded him; she wasn't going to hang up on him, despite the twenty questions.

"He's my best friend at work." Cal paused, then sighed, then paused again. "And it was so I wouldn't drunk-text you."

Brenna's peal of delighted laughter was the best sound in the fucking world. This—*this*—was what he'd been missing. Not the sex—well, that too—but the closeness. These shared moments in the darkness, making each other laugh.

Now all he needed was her, next to him. Her warmth. Her scent. His hands buried in the slippery silk of her hair. The rhythmic gusts of her breath tickling his neck as she slept, wrapped securely in his arms.

"Christ, Bren. I miss you so much," he choked out. And promptly regretted it, when his confession brought her laughter to an immediate halt. But he pressed onward. "I miss falling asleep with you. I haven't been able to sleep properly since…the last time I saw you."

He could hear her breathing, but her silence continued.

"Say something, Bren. Say anything. Please," he begged. "Just…talk to me."

There was a long pause before she finally responded. "What should we talk about?"

Again, the sick feeling of relief, of disaster averted, was overwhelming.

"Anything. Anything. About your week. About how things are going with Serenity Massage. You were sleeping, right? Maybe we could both lie here on our pillows and talk to each other as we fall asleep. Like we used to. I really miss that."

More inane babbling. Incredibly, she was willing to humor him.

"The business is going really well. August was my best month in ages. I'm thinking of raising my rates for the first time in more than two years. And then I might be able to cut back my schedule a little."

"That's great!" He hoped it also meant she wasn't skipping lunch so frequently. But he didn't dare disturb their fragile connection by asking.

"I'm getting some new clients, too. Someone bought a ten-pack of gift certificates a few weeks ago and gave them to her friends, apparently."

Cal's lips curved in a secret smile. "Good."

"How was the wedding?"

"Fine, I suppose. Spent most of the reception at the hotel bar."

"Why?" she asked, sounding baffled and faintly horrified.

His reply was low and intimate, prodding her. "You know why."

When she didn't respond, he continued. "I didn't want to drag anyone else down with me. Weddings are supposed to be happy, aren't they?"

"Oh, Cal." The wealth of compassion in her voice was almost more than he could bear. It was certainly more than he deserved. Even now that they weren't together anymore, she still empathized with his misery. And when they *had* been together, she'd done everything in her power to comfort and encourage him, emotionally and physically.

And how had he treated her? First he'd tried to shove her into the friends-with-benefits box along with all the other girls he'd been involved with over the years. She'd accepted those boundaries—up to a point. And afterward, he'd still tried to compartmentalize his relationship with her, keeping it completely separate from the rest of his life.

He had treated her so unfairly.

"Let's talk about something else," he said, his voice gruff with suppressed emotion.

"Of course."

As she told him about Ash and Cissy's housewarming party, Cal slowly relaxed. His heavy eyelids slid shut. Her voice was just so soothing…

"Cal?"

"Hmm?"

"You're falling asleep, aren't you?"

"Mmph." The corners of his lips twitched at her good-humored accusation.

"I'll hang up, this call is probably costing you seventy-five million dollars."

He yawned. "Best seventy-five million I ever spent."

She chuckled. "Night, Cal."

"Night, Bren."

He drifted off with the phone cradled against his ear and a sappy grin still stretching his cheeks.

In lieu of his eight a.m. alarm, he was awoken the next morning by a grouchy Jordie, bitterly complaining about assholes who refused to sleep in on weekends. Then the offending item—Cal's phone—was tossed unceremoni-ously onto the bed, smacking his shin on the rebound and wiping the amusement off his face.

"Ow! What was that for?"

"It didn't even work anyway, did it?" Jordie jerked his chin at the incriminating handset on Cal's pillow. "You drunk-dialed her from the hotel phone—which, by the way, you're paying me back for. I'm not subsidizing your descent into madness."

Cal struggled to a sitting position, his back against the headboard. "Such drama." He started to shake his head in mock disapproval but halted the jarring movement with a wince. "Look, the call went…well." Last night's sappy grin threatened to reappear despite his pounding head, as he remembered the thrill of simply hearing Brenna's voice again after so long. "Anyway, sorry my alarm woke you." He hoped he sounded at least semi-sincere. "I've got a plane to catch in a few hours. I'm heading up to New Hampshire for the rest of the weekend."

"Fine, whatever," Jordie grumbled, crossing the room to his suitcase. "I'm meeting Lara and some of the others for breakfast in forty-five minutes. Wanna join us?"

"As long as the flirting stays within manageable proportions."

"Won't be a problem," his friend said matter-of-factly.

Cal arched a brow as Jordie headed to the bathroom. But since Lara was a coworker, he wasn't going to ask, and he was pretty sure Jordie wasn't going to tell. He hoped for Jordie's sake any awkwardness would be short-lived.

Two Advil, one perfunctory breakfast—at a table populated by half a dozen hungover attorneys—and six hours later, Cal was nearing the Craftsman-style house on the shore of Baxter Lake. He had caught the shuttle to Logan, firmly ignoring the instinct to grab a cab over to Brenna's place. Instead, he'd rented a car for the ninety-minute drive north, forcing himself to escape from her gravity well as quickly as possible.

Most of the block was already full of cars when he arrived, as was the driveway. So he pulled past and parked half a block down, leaving his overnight bag in the trunk.

Armed with a smile and a six-pack of his brother-in-law Tom's favorite honey brown ale, he followed the piquant scents of charbroiled chicken and steak up the wide driveway. He passed the familiar fieldstone and exposed-beam facade, taking the flagstone path around to the grassy backyard and the deck overlooking the sparkling lake below.

His niece and nephew were the first to spot him. Their joyous shrieks of "Uncle Cal!" drew the attention of the rest of his family, and a crowd soon surrounded him. It took a solid ten minutes of hugs, handshakes, and congratulatory back-slaps before he was finally able to make himself a plate of food and snag a beer from the cooler. His mom was over the moon that he'd showed up; every time he looked in her direction, she was smiling at him. Cal was glad he'd made the trip.

And yet, as the party wound down and he stood nursing a beer and staring out across the gradually darkening lake at the pearlescent sky, he found himself wishing again that Brenna were with him. Even here, at such a great distance from the orbit of his daily life, her gravitational pull drew his thoughts unerringly toward her.

Today would have been the perfect opportunity to introduce her to his family. Maybe her presence would have also eased the grief he was never quite able to suppress when he visited the lake house.

"Something on your mind?" his mom asked. He glanced to his left, where she'd quietly sidled up next to him. She now wore a dark green fleece pullover against the evening chill, reminding him that he was still dressed for a warm summer's day. He needed to pull his car into the driveway at some point and grab his overnight bag.

"Would I be crazy to put in for a transfer to CMH's Boston office?"

"What? Where's this coming from? Not that I wouldn't be thrilled to have you back in New England."

"Well…" He stalled, debating how much to tell her, then decided to go all in. "Over the summer, I was seeing this girl in Boston. Brenna. She broke up with me a few weeks ago, and I haven't been able to stop thinking about her."

His mom's brows went up, and he hastily added, "It's not just about her, though. A lot of my clients are in the Boston area. And I'd also like to live closer to you, and Megan and Tom and the kids. I never see you guys," he said with a wry twist of his lips.

"I don't even know where to start unpacking all of that, so I'm going to start with the girl you never once mentioned before." She frowned at him, the very picture of offended maternal concern. "Brenna, you said?"

He nodded.

"Tell me what's so special about her."

"Everything," he said fervently. "She's warm, and compassionate, and caring. And smart. And hardworking. And gorgeous. And she makes me laugh."

He stopped listing Brenna's virtues when he noticed the smile that had crept onto his mom's face, crinkling the corners of her blue eyes. "What?"

"I can't tell you how long I've waited for you to really fall for someone, Cal. I thought you'd never give me grandchildren, but—"

"Hey! It's a bit early to be counting the grandkids, Mom," he admonished her, even as the idea warmed him from the inside out.

"Well, look. About this transfer idea. My vote is going to be yes, regardless, but aren't you worried that transferring so soon after you made partner might have an impact on your career?"

He was, but the idea he had in mind represented a positive impact, rather than a negative one—assuming he could persuade CMH to support it. He needed advice, but he didn't want to approach anyone at the firm before his path was certain.

Cal sighed. "I wish Dad were here."

Wrapping an arm around his waist, his mom squeezed him to her side. "I know you do, honey. I still miss him, too, every day. He would have been so proud that you made partner." She glanced at him. "But after he got sick, he also wanted to make sure you understood that some things are more important than work."

"I do. I get it now."

"I'm really glad you came up today. It makes me so happy to have all of my family with me." Then she took a step back and faced him square-on, clasping his hand in her delicate fingers. "Sort things out with Brenna, okay? Because I want to meet her."

"I'm working on it."

"What does she do, by the way? You didn't say."

He looked her in the eye, unflinching. "She's a massage therapist. She's got her own business on Newbury Street."

"A massage therapist." Her expression grew calculating. "We could definitely use one of those in the family…"

"Mo—om." He drew out the word in mock exasperation.

"I'm just saying. My back's been hurting lately—you could always give your old mom a gift certificate."

"Funny you should mention that. Coincidentally, I happen to have bought a bunch of them a couple of weeks ago."

"You did, did you?" Her eyes lit up. "Then one of them must be for me, right?"

There was no way out of it, so he capitulated as gracefully as he could. "Of course. But it may be a while before I can give it to you. I kind of have something planned."

"You always have something planned, sweetheart. That's why you've been so successful. My son, the partner." She beamed at him, then pulled him into a fierce hug. "Congratulations again, honey."

"Thanks, Mom."

Then she whispered in his ear, "Now, get to work on those grandchildren."

He smiled. *All in good time.*

13

BRENNA WOKE ON FRIDAY filled with anticipation. What would today's present be? After Cal's late-night confessional last Saturday, her expectations were high. He hadn't called since then, but he'd sent a text Monday night saying he hadn't stopped missing her the entire weekend. They'd texted or e-mailed every day since.

His *Good morning, beautiful* message buoyed her sense of well-being through the late afternoon. But as the day wound down with no further sign or word from him, her good mood began to slip. First to irritation. Then to anxiety. And eventually to resigned disappointment, as she prepped the suite after her final client had left.

She was tidying the large therapy room when the doorbell chimed, precisely at her new—and earlier—weekend closing time. She frowned. Who'd be stopping by at eight o'clock?

As she approached the suite's glass door to let her visitor in, her mouth fell open.

Perhaps the long, presentless day had robbed her of her mental faculties. She blinked once, twice. Nope, still there. Maybe she should eat another of Cal's snack bars. Though skipping lunch had never brought on hallucinations before.

Impressively realistic, the figment of her imagination had a colorful bouquet in one hand, a white paper shopping bag in the other, and an expression somewhere between incredulous and awestruck on his face.

With shaking hands, Brenna unlocked and opened the door.

"I can't believe I'm actually seeing you, right here in front of me," said a familiar husky baritone.

Okaaay. Not a figment. Her stomach dropped out like a car on a roller-coaster, and she staggered back a few steps. "Cal? Wh—what are you doing here?"

He straightened, somehow managing to look simultaneously apologetic and defiant. Not to mention breathtakingly gorgeous in dark blue chinos and a short-sleeved button-down shirt that had her attention riveted to the triangle of tanned skin exposed at the top of his chest.

"It's closing time," he said, "and I'm here to take you to dinner. If you'll let me."

Cal had just thrown down the present-giving gauntlet.

She took a step toward him. The appreciative heat in his gaze wasn't searing her with lust, this time. His gray eyes shone instead with warmth and devotion. And she knew, if she turned him away without at least giving him a chance, she would regret it for the rest of her life.

She said one word: "Yes."

Pure joy spread across his face as if she'd answered another question entirely.

Drawing closer to him, she smiled in return. "Let me see if I have a vase for the flowers—"

"No need." He held up the paper bag.

"Ah, there's my Eagle Scout. Always prepared."

"I aim to please," he said lightly, his usual hint of cocky smugness absent. "Looks like you need a few more minutes to finish up, and I know you need to get changed. Anything I can do to help?" His tentative question nearly melted her heart.

She held out her hands for the flowers and vase. Time to put that ikebana class she'd taken with her mom to good use.

"How about if you strip the rest of the linens from the table in here and the other therapy room. You can put them in the laundry bag in the front closet. Fresh sheets are in the cabinet over there," she indicated, inclining her head, "and by the time you've got the fitted sheets on the tables I should be back."

Brenna brushed past him in search of some scissors, too flustered to wait for his agreement. She needed a few minutes to process that, unbelievably, Cal was *here*, smelling amazing and looking even more incredible than she'd remembered.

It took her about five minutes to disassemble and re-arrange the bouquet into the thick, hand-blown glass vase in a pleasing manner. Feeling calmer, she set the arrangement on the side table in the cozy reception area where her clients could enjoy it while they waited for their appointments. The bonsai Cal had given her would have to go in the larger therapy room for now.

A new fitted sheet was already on the massage table in there, and a folded flat sheet and blanket were stacked precisely in the middle of it. So she called out to him, "I'm going to get changed now, if that's okay."

"Of course," came his muffled reply from the second,

smaller therapy room. "Take your time."

The warm early September morning had spurred her to put on a long, cotton dress with an oversized floral print that would thankfully be suitable at pretty much any restaurant. She brought it into the large therapy room and, after a brief hesitation, decided not to lock the door. He wasn't a stranger, and she knew he had too much respect for her to ever barge in. But she still felt vulnerable as she changed out of her uniform—which was not what she'd ever imagined wearing in any fantasized reunion scenario.

She swapped her clogs for strappy leather sandals, shoved her soiled uniform into a laundry bag, and, with a racing heartbeat, went to meet her destiny.

He bent over the table in the other therapy room as he tugged the last corner of the sheet into place. Holy crap, the man had a truly magnificent ass. Brenna's teeth sank into her lower lip as she admired his backside for a second or two, a welcome jolt of heat rushing through her.

Tempting as the thought was, if she spent the entire night staring at his remarkable...glutes, she knew they would never get out of there. So she stepped up beside him and, working together, they had the suite prepped in another five minutes.

They were soon strolling down Newbury Street toward L'Avenue—she was lucky indeed, tonight. Then again, so was he.

"It's a good thing I wore something today that's dressy enough for L'Avenue," she said, trying to inject a playful tone into their conversation. "What would you have done if it had been ninety degrees and I'd been wearing short shorts, a tank top, and flip flops?"

He looked at her, and the stark need reflected in his eyes created her own personal heat wave. But then he banked that scorching heat down to a manageable smolder and said, "I had a backup plan." He smiled with a trace of his usual cockiness. "But I'm glad I didn't have to use it."

Out of habit her hand slid into his, and he twined their fingers together. Cal matched his longer stride to her shorter one, the back of his hand occasionally brushing her hip as they walked in step.

She knew they would have to clear the air before they could get back together. And she was not at all looking forward to it. The prospect of make-up sex, definitely yes. The process of making up, not so much.

During dinner, Cal continued to steer them toward lighter topics. He might have thought he was doing her a favor by avoiding any unpleasantness—after all, why ruin a spectacular meal with a difficult conversation? But her nerves were jangling so hard she was barely able to swallow a few mouthfuls of her pan-fried trout or the accompanying barley and wild rice pilaf or roasted asparagus spears.

Their plates were cleared, and she half-heartedly prolonged her torture with an order of chamomile tea and a plum *tarte tatin*.

While they awaited their desserts, Cal took her hands in his. To her relief and consternation, he said, "Bren, I've done a lot of thinking over the past month."

He paused for so long she wondered if he were awaiting a response. But then he went on, saying the words she'd been hoping to hear pretty much since day one. "The truth is, I'm crazy about you. No more friends-with-benefits. You deserve more," he said earnestly. "We both do."

She wasn't quite ready to admit she was crazy about him, too. "But what about being embarrassed by me?" It still bothered her that he'd felt that way.

He glanced away for a moment, then caught her gaze again with renewed intensity. "I still feel awful that I tried to keep our relationship separate from the rest of my life. And even worse that I made you feel bad. It's not an excuse, but I was worried about the partnership decision at the time and... Well, it was stupid, and I regret it. I was never embarrassed by you or what you do for a living. And I hope you can forgive me."

"So you're not going to hide me from your colleagues or family anymore?"

"I've already told everyone who matters. My mom can't wait to meet you."

Brenna couldn't help it; her eyebrows rose in tandem with her speeding heart rate.

"Jordie's just looking forward to when I stop moping, as he put it. Though he's gonna be pissed when he finds out I've asked for a transfer to the Boston office."

"You did *what?*"

"Don't freak out." His thumbs rubbed delicate, soothing circles against the backs of her trembling hands. "I've been considering it for a while now, since even before I met you."

Their server arrived with their desserts. Brenna took a bite of hers, followed by a sip of her too-hot tea, trying to quell her panic. This was too much, too fast. But Cal always seemed to see through her so easily it was a safe bet he'd know she was, indeed, freaking out.

"Why do you want to move up here?" she asked, hoping to forestall Cal's questions about how the idea made her feel.

"Lots of reasons."

And since he was a lawyer, she knew he would enumerate them all.

"First, my family is still in Portsmouth." He told her about wanting to spend more time with his niece and nephew and be nearer to his aging mother, and her heartbeat began to slow as he described this first, perfectly reasonable—in fact, admirable—motivation.

He added another one to the list. "Second, work." Wanting to better serve his New England-based clients also made sense, and his ambition to start a litigation department in Boston for his firm impressed her. Maybe this was just a happy coincidence of purposes.

"And that brings me to my third reason," he said, his focus squarely on her. "You."

Her heart leapt right back into her throat.

"I want to see if we can do this for real, not just on weekends. It would make all the difference knowing we could be with each other every day, if we want to. I know I want to."

He swallowed before continuing, his emotions clearly running high. "It just feels right." Softly, he asked her, "Does it feel like the right thing to you, too?"

It was where she'd hoped they would end up all along. A wellspring of joy began to bubble up, but she capped it, wanting to make sure she understood what he was suggesting first. "It does, but... You're just talking about moving to Boston, not moving in with me, right?"

He laughed. "Of course I'm not planning to just move in with you. Oh my God, that would be so presumptuous."

"Yeah, I thought so, too," she said as relief gave way to playfulness. "But best to make sure, you know?"

"Finish up that dessert, babe," he prodded, his eyes darkening like a summer storm. Apparently he was eager to get to the make-up sex, too.

She took another bite, letting the complex flavors spread across her tongue. Now that she seemed to have survived making up with Cal, she could enjoy the tartness of the plums paired with the cool, spicy sweetness of the cinnamon ice cream. The sugar rush helped dampen the lingering aftereffects of her anxiety, too.

"Want a taste of mine?" Cal offered her a spoonful of his triple-chocolate mousse, along with a lashing of the Grand Marnier whipped cream that accompanied it.

She accepted it, throatily humming her approval. "I should've gotten that one. The chocolate is just so...intense."

"If it does that to you, I'm more than happy to trade." His voice was as rich and velvety as the mousse. "As long as you let me watch you eat it."

"I wouldn't mind another bite."

He offered her another spoonful, his own lips parted with anticipation.

Her eyelids fluttered shut as she took the spoon between her lips. As he withdrew it, she moaned softly. Truthfully, she was hamming it up a bit, though it really was one of the most incredible things she'd ever tasted.

"Okay, we're going now." He abruptly signaled their server.

"But these desserts are so good," she protested, her eyes dancing as he asked for the bill.

"You can finish up while I get the check."

She took another bite of her own dessert, waving her spoon at him. "Culinary masterpieces like these are meant to be savored, not wolfed down."

"I'm feeling pretty wolfish, right about now."

Brenna's wanton side finally resurfaced after a month in hibernation. She leaned toward him. "Are you hard for me, baby?" she cooed.

"I've been hard for you since the day I met you," he muttered, looking around. "Where the hell is that check?"

"While we're waiting, I think I'll have another bite of this gorgeous plum tart." She slipped the spoon between her lips, licking off a trace of ice cream suggestively. "Mmm. You want a taste?"

Cal looked about ready to lunge across the table and sample the dessert from her lips. Her nipples hardened at the thought of his imminent loss of control.

He noticed—of course he did. "Ohhh, Brenna, don't do this to me." His leg jiggled up and down against her knee in his agitation.

Their server finally appeared with the check. Cal immediately sent her off with his credit card, telling her they were in a hurry. Understatement of the century.

Brenna arched her back slightly, pushing her small breasts out so they strained against the fabric of her dress.

Cal was captivated by the display. "You are so gonna get it when we get home."

"That's good," she retorted. "'Cause I really, really need it."

The sound that came out of the back of his throat sounded remarkably like a growl, and her eyes widened. Then she noticed his flared nostrils and the perspiration dampening his temples. He looked like an enraged bull who'd scented his mate in the next paddock and was ready to break through the fence separating them. Oopsie. Maybe she'd gone overboard with the teasing?

His command was gritted out from between clenched teeth. "Not. Another. Word."

She smiled coyly, but said nothing as he paid the check. He'd find out soon enough how wet she already was for him. Turning this controlled, confident man into a quivering mass of testosterone and lust was going to become one of her favorite pastimes.

In short order he had bundled her into a cab, trying to keep his distance during the ride as he attempted to restore his self-control. His rangy frame radiated a taut urgency. She placed a soothing hand on his upper thigh— well, she'd intended it to be soothing, at any rate.

Before she could process what was happening, he'd engulfed her in his embrace. His tongue slid into her mouth, and he thumbed her nipple as his palm caressed her breast.

Her hand cupped his erection, which jumped beneath her touch. She just bet it was covered with slippery precome, all warm and musky and smelling of Cal.

She might have moaned. Cal definitely did.

It didn't take long before they arrived at Brenna's apartment. When they broke apart, panting and breathless, his pupils were blown, leaving just a rim of smoky silver remaining around the edges.

He practically threw a twenty at the cabbie as he ushered her out of the back seat. She held the foyer door open for him, then launched herself up the three flights of stairs, knowing he'd be close behind.

At the top, she struggled to unlock her door. It wasn't helping that every single inch of his erection was pressed up against her butt, while his fingers curled possessively around her hips.

"Cal, you're just going to make me take longer," she protested in a quavering voice. He merely bent down and started nibbling and sucking on the sweet spot along the tendon in her neck. She shivered, her fine motor skills deserting her.

Finally they burst through the door, slamming it behind them as they rushed for the sofa, clothes and shoes flying everywhere. The bedroom was simply too far away and their need was too great.

He urged her onto her knees, and she braced her hands against the sofa's back, her hair cascading over one shoulder as she looked up at him behind her. In this position, her thighs were spread and her buttocks tilted upward. She trembled with desire, imagining Cal seeing her pussy all soft, and open, and wet.

Without a word he rolled on a condom—prepared, as always—and mounted her. Lining up the head of his cock against her, he drove it home, spearing deep into her with a tortured groan. Within a few strokes, his rhythm had become fast and hard, accompanied by little grunts of effort.

Oh yeah, her bull had busted through the paddock fence, all right.

Her head dropped down. She reached for her swollen clit, busily working it as Cal pounded into her.

"Christ, Bren," he panted. "You feel so fuckin' good."

Brenna rubbed faster, the strain in his voice spurring her on. Her orgasm was building, and his big, warm body suddenly covered her, the slightly roughened pad of his finger displacing hers. She let out a whimper at the burst of pure pleasure catalyzed by his touch.

His next words were strangled, incoherent. "I'm not... I can't..."

The idea of Cal robbed of the power of speech nearly blinded her with lust. Her arousal spiked as she tumbled into an orgasm, shrieking as it ripped through her.

"Oh my God!" he exclaimed. Then his hot mouth was on her neck as he shuddered and moaned his climax against her skin.

They remained there like that for a minute, Cal's breath puffing against the back of her shoulder between the kisses he nuzzled onto her.

"That was amazing," he said. "You're amazing." He gently pulled out of her and dealt with the condom. Then he eased onto the sofa and guided her into his lap, bringing them chest to chest, skin to skin.

She straddled his muscular thighs, and his arms immediately came around her, crushing her to him in the most wonderful way. With his dear, handsome face cupped in her hands, she kissed him—mouth, cheeks, jaw, neck, mouth again—desperately trying to erase the weeks they'd been apart.

"Ah, Bren," he murmured. "I need you so much."

"Need you, too," she said between kisses.

His embrace eased, and his hands began softly tracing up and down her back. "Not just for sex. For everything."

"I know. Me too."

And then his arms wrapped her up again, so tight there was barely room to breathe.

"I want so badly to say, 'Let's not fight again,' and for you to agree," he said. "But I know that's not realistic."

He pulled back, and his eyes were clear, his expression earnest. "So instead I'm going to say, let's not break up again, when we fight. Let's talk about whatever it is, and work it out. Because I think we're really good together."

Despite being more practical than romantic, his words gave her a rush of confidence in their future. "I agree," she said with a smile. "Wanna seal it with a kiss?"

Cal nodded, his own smile turning mischievous. "Though we still have a serious kiss deficit from last month."

"Then we'd better get cracking." And she bent her face to his, dropping the first of those kisses onto his soft, sweet lips.

14

"Bren!" Cal called over his shoulder in the direction of the bathroom door. "Come out of there, I don't want us to be late. And I want to see you in that dress."

He was already in his tux, silver cuff links gleaming from his French cuffs. He frowned at his hair in the mirror. Maybe Brenna could help him style it. If she ever came out of the bathroom, that is.

She'd refused to let him see the dress she'd bought for the Partner Prom, though she'd revealed what color it was—champagne blush, whatever that meant. He imagined her clad in frothy bubbles. He imagined licking frothy bubbles off all of his favorite places—the spot on the side of her neck that made her shiver; the fine, slightly paler skin at the top of her throat; her rose-petal soft inner thighs; around and around each dusky nipple...

He started guiltily when the bathroom door clicked open and Brenna made her grand entrance.

"Oh my gosh, look at you!" she enthused.

He'd completely forgotten he was wearing a tuxedo. Because she was poured into a lustrous pale pink gown that slid like silk over her curves. Two tiny straps held the dress up at each shoulder. An off-center slit up the front revealed a breathtaking glimpse of her long, toned legs.

And holy hell, she wore sexy stiletto heels that he knew he'd be telling her to leave on when he finally gave in and hustled her back to their hotel room later that night.

He'd seen her in plenty of dresses before, but never a dress like this. She was the picture of confident, stylish elegance. Yet at the same time, she'd never looked sexier.

His gaze lifted to hers once more. He regarded her helplessly, digging deep for the words to express how she looked. How she made him feel.

"Wow," he breathed.

Those gorgeous, golden brown eyes sparkled with mischief. "You haven't even seen the back yet." And she pirouetted a half-turn.

He groaned. "Oh my God, Bren. You're killing me."

The dress scooped low, plunging nearly to her waist. In a miracle of engineering, the two straps at each shoulder criss-crossed her upper back, holding the otherwise backless dress close to her body.

He wanted to keep her all to himself in their luxury hotel room's king-sized bed, warm and naked. Except for those fuck-me shoes; they could stay on.

He wanted to show her off, introduce her to Jordie so maybe the man would finally understand why he had to move to Boston.

He wanted to shout to the world that she was *his,* and no one else's.

Brenna swung back to face him. "Didn't you say we were going to be late?" Her smug grin was adorable. She could clearly tell the effect she had on him, and she was enjoying it immensely.

"Yes," he managed to croak. Time no longer mattered,

however.

She crossed her arms, which merely plumped her luscious little breasts up above the dress's draping neckline. "Cal, I took a day and a half off from work for this. I don't want to miss dinner."

He shook his head, regaining his senses. Of course they couldn't miss dinner.

"Right." He paused to collect his scattered thoughts. "Can you do something with my hair? It's not working."

She looked him up and down like the vixen she usually hid inside. "I dunno, that bed-head vibe you've got going works pretty darned well for me."

"Bren, you know I can't go down there like this. You can mess my hair up all you want after it's over."

"Trust me, I will," she assured him as she sat him down in the desk chair.

Five minutes later she'd worked some kind of magic he was pretty sure he could never replicate on his own, and his hair looked perfect. But Brenna was still missing something, he remembered as he stood up.

"You're not ready," he said.

"Yes, I am," she insisted.

"You look...unadorned."

"What?"

"Allow me to take care of that for you." And he pulled a small rectangular jewelry box out of his pocket.

"Cal," she protested delightedly, "you didn't need to do that."

"Open it," was all he said.

He'd spent several weeks looking for exactly the right present. After seeing her in that dress, with loose tendrils escaping from her upswept hair, he was even more certain he'd chosen wisely.

She lifted the box's lid to reveal round diamond studs set in white gold, each with a little chain attached to a dangling barely-pink freshwater pearl. "Cal, they're beautiful." Her eyes shone when they met his. "Thank you."

"It's my pleasure," he said, and meant it.

She put the earrings on, then tilted her face up for a kiss.

He meant to give her just a chaste brush of the lips. But she melted against him, her lips parting, and he couldn't resist sliding the tip of his tongue between them. She moaned softly into his mouth, her tongue tip flicking against his, and his hands came around her upper back, pressing against the silkiness of bare skin. He tugged her closer, settling the cradle of her hips against his groin.

It would be so easy to lay her down on that huge expanse of a bed. Surely they could miss part of the cocktail hour without raising too many eyebrows. Couldn't they?

Cal knew better, much as he wished he didn't.

Reluctantly, he pulled away, breathing hard. Brenna's lipstick had somehow remained unsmudged, but her lips were swollen from his kisses, and it made him all kinds of crazy.

"Now we're both ready," he said, though his pulse still raced. "Nervous?"

"A little." She took his arm. "I'm also kind of excited. I like getting all dressed up, and it's been a long time since I've had a reason to."

"I like you getting all dressed up, too," he said with a waggle of his eyebrows, covering her hand with his own.

He escorted her up to the spectacular high-ceilinged ballroom foyer, where cocktails were already being served. The mood was festive. Hundreds of formally dressed attorneys and their guests milled around, greeted each other, and made heavy inroads into the well-stocked open bar.

They found a smaller bar on one side of the room, where the press of guests was only three deep. Joining them in line were Jordie and Lara, who—to Cal's surprise—had accompanied each other to the event. Cal was enormously pleased to introduce Brenna to them as his girlfriend.

The foursome chatted while they waited to order their drinks. When Lara was busy admiring Brenna's new earrings, Jordie gave Cal a surreptitious thumbs-up.

Then he leaned closer to Cal. "Golden unicorn, dude," Jordie whispered hoarsely, shaking his head in disbelieving approval.

This time, Cal refused to pass up the opportunity to ask, "What does that even mean?"

The reply was typical Jordie—surprisingly deep, overlaid with his quirky sense of humor. "Something so rare and wonderful you can't believe it actually exists."

Well, that certainly summed up Brenna.

Cal nodded, conceding the point. He still sometimes couldn't quite believe they'd ended up together, or that what they had was so special.

After an eternity, they got their drinks and were free to mingle with the crowd. Since Brenna and Lara had hit it off, the four agreed to meet up again for dinner. Jordie insisted they should sit near the stage, but refused to explain why.

His reason became clear as they waited for the dessert course to be served. CMH's managing partner stepped up to the microphone and spoke for several minutes about the firm's key successes in the previous year and its rosy prospects for the next one. Then he congratulated all the new partners and, one by one, called them up to the stage to introduce them to the rest of the partnership.

At least Cal had some warning, since his name was at the end of the alphabet. He felt a bit bad for Tiffany Alaki, who looked both honored and charmingly shell-shocked when she crossed the stage to shake the managing partner's hand and receive the applause of her peers, almost like a graduation ceremony. Which wasn't a bad analogy, when he considered it further in the minutes before his own name was called.

By the time he sat down again, the eleven-piece band had struck up some jazzy background music, and dessert and coffee had been served. Cal eyed the plates in front of him and Brenna with mild alarm—the slices of cake looked very layered and very, very chocolatey.

"I wanted to wait 'til you got back before I tasted it," Brenna said. The flirtatious undertone in her seemingly polite statement was clearly for his benefit.

"Are you sure you want to eat that?"

"It's chocolate. Of course I'm going to eat it."

"Bren," he warned with a smile.

"What?" She was all innocence.

Until she slipped the fork between her full, pink lips. He couldn't tear his eyes away as her eyelids closed sensually. She swallowed, the column of her throat gently convulsing.

Then she opened her eyes and turned to him. "Not bad. But it's not even in the same universe as the chocolate mousse at L'Avenue." She broke off a morsel, then offered her fork to him. "Here, you try it."

"I've got my own," he said, so she ate it herself. He bent his head to her ear and whispered, "Tease."

She swallowed her bite of cake, then she leaned toward him. "Wait 'til we're back in our room. I'll show you some teasing," she purred.

Just like that his eyes unfocused, and all the blood in his body surged straight to his groin.

"I wish you hadn't said that. I was going to ask you to dance, but now I need to wait a few minutes."

"You poor thing." She patted his knee, her eyes gleaming. "I'll try a little harder not to be so sexy."

"That is un-possible," he muttered.

She laughed, but it only made him want to kiss her more.

Averting his eyes from her temptations, Cal scanned the crowd and noticed Grant and his wife headed toward him. Now, there was a welcome distraction if ever he needed one.

Grant parked himself between Cal and Brenna, one hand resting on each chair back, and bent down to be heard over the music and chatter.

"Cal, you remember my wife, Beth?"

"Of course." Cal nodded a greeting at her over Grant's shoulder, unable to move his chair without dislodging Grant.

"No, no, don't stand up," Grant said. "I just wanted to

say hello." He turned to the other side. "And you must be Brenna. I heard a lot about you when Cal approached me about transferring to Boston. All good things," he assured her with a smile.

"Bren, this is Grant," Cal said. "I was up in Boston with him for the trial back in May."

"Oh!" She twisted in her seat, offering her hand for him to shake. "You must be the boss. I guess I should thank you. I don't think Cal and I would have met, if it wasn't for you."

Grant raised his bushy brows. "The boss, eh? I like it." His head swiveled back to Cal. "Well, I don't want to keep the two of you from your dessert. Beth and I will see you on the dance floor later, right?"

"Absolutely," Cal said.

Grant shifted over two seats to Cal's right and leaned down to schmooze with Lara and Jordie, leaving Beth standing beside him with good-natured patience.

"They're so cute," Brenna said, turning to Cal. "His pocket square matches her dress."

He glanced to the side. So it did. "I could try to do that next year, if you wanted."

"Maybe. I kind of liked surprising you though," she said with a coy smile.

"Then maybe you could buy the matching pocket square."

"Okay," she agreed, evidently pleased with the idea.

It thrilled him to talk so casually with her about the future, as if it was a foregone conclusion they would be together. They'd still have to work at their relationship, of course. But it was reassuring to know that at least they shared the same intention.

The band started playing a cover of Norah Jones's "Come Away with Me," and Cal knew the time was right. "Have you had enough of your inferior chocolate dessert?" he teased. "I want to dance with you. We've never danced."

She set her fork down and briefly pressed her napkin to her lips. "It's hard to say no to you, when you're so eager."

He'd have to remember that.

He stood, then pulled out Brenna's chair as he helped her to her feet. They were only a few steps from the dance floor. "You wouldn't happen to know how to waltz, by any chance?"

"I took social dancing for a semester in college," she said dubiously, "but that was a long time ago…"

"Excellent." And he swung her expertly around to face him, her left hand coming to rest on his right shoulder.

Her eyes locked on his. "Oooh, you know how to do this. I can tell."

"I know how to do lots of things," he said with a mischievous smile, before guiding her into the first steps of the pattern. She was very responsive to his lead, he noted with pleasure, as he swirled her around the dance floor as if they'd been partners for years.

Everyone applauded the band when the song ended. "That was wonderful!" Brenna told him, clapping her hands. "You were already off-the-charts amazing even before I knew you could dance. You just earned *so* many bonus points."

He was about to respond when someone a few feet away from them shouted Brenna's name. They both turned. Waving madly at them was a woman Cal didn't recognize, dragging along a bemused-looking man Cal knew—Doug, a corporate partner in the Boston office whom Cal had reached out to several weeks ago, before his transfer.

"Brenna, it's so unbelievable you're here! You look gorgeous, by the way. And the way the two of you danced, wow! I thought I was watching *Dancing with the Stars*," the woman gushed. She turned to Cal. "Hi, I'm Julie, Doug's wife."

"Cal Wilcox." He shook her offered hand.

"Welcome to Boston, Cal." Then, like a swallow in flight, Julie turned the conversation again. "Doug, this is Brenna, my new massage therapist. She is the *best*. Brenna, this is my husband, Doug."

"Nice to meet you." Brenna nodded at Doug, who hadn't managed to get a word in edgewise.

"I didn't know your boyfriend worked at CMH," Julie said. "That's such a coincidence!"

Brenna arched a brow. "It is indeed." She turned to Cal, her tone dripping with exaggerated surprise. "Right, honey?"

Luckily, she waited to commence her interrogation of him until after Julie had dragged Doug off to "dance to her favorite song!"

Hands on hips, Brenna drawled, "So you're the 'Mrs. Truesdale' who bought those gift certificates, I presume?"

"No…"

She frowned at him, awaiting an explanation of his unspoken "not quite."

He 'fessed up. "Well, I kind of borrowed my sister

Megan's name."

"Ha!" Then she blinked. "Let me get this straight. I broke up with you, and three days later you dropped a thousand dollars on gift certificates for Serenity Massage. That's just...wow." She shook her head. "What if we hadn't gotten back together?"

There wasn't really a good answer to that question. So he shrugged and said with a cocky grin, "I'm an optimist?"

"Cal," she said, lengthening his name exasperatedly. She wasn't done grilling him, either. "So the energy bars weren't actually my first present then, either."

"Yes, they were."

"But you bought the gift certificates the day before I got the energy bars."

"I don't consider the gift certificates to be a present. They were for Serenity Massage. Everything else was for you."

Her brow crinkled adorably. "You bought Serenity Massage a present?"

He considered her question. "I suppose you could think of it that way. You'd said you wanted someone who supported your career and cared about your business. So I tried to do that. I gave the gift certificates to people I thought might be good additions to your clientele. I figured, you know, maybe some of them would become repeat clients or tell their friends, or something."

"They did." She paused thoughtfully. "Your present has already been more successful than some of my formal marketing campaigns. It's really making a difference."

Pride swelled warmly in his chest. This was ten times better than making partner.

Brenna rose onto her tiptoes and brushed her lips across his. "Thank you, sweetie."

As he gazed at her with nothing short of adoration, it was right on the tip of his tongue to tell her he loved her. He didn't really know why he was still holding back at this point, and it would be hard to find a more perfect moment than this one. Or, for that matter, a more perfectly memorable occasion, dressed to the nines under the scintillating chandeliers of the Waldorf's Starlight Roof.

But he'd barely moved up to Boston a month ago, and it still seemed too soon. Besides, Brenna had only ever made that one, offhand reference to loving him—she'd never said the actual words. He didn't want to put pressure on her to say it back to him if she wasn't ready. And honestly, he wasn't sure *he* was ready to put that particular label on his feelings, because even though things were going really well, he'd never felt this way before, and what if he jinxed them—

She looked up at him with shining eyes and, thankfully, took the choice right out of his hands. "I love you, Cal."

"I love you too, Bren. So much," he told her, imbuing his words with every ounce of the emotion brimming over in his heart.

Right there in the middle of the dance floor, in front of three hundred of his esteemed colleagues and their guests, Cal kissed her—long, and slow, and chocolatey sweet.

And he didn't give a damn who saw them.

EXCERPT FROM
AN INTERNATIONAL AFFAIR

Keep reading for an excerpt from the next book in Alexa's sizzling-hot BigLaw Romance series, *An International Affair*.

(Coming soon!)

1

"OI. SHANE."

Shane Tracy didn't even have to look up from his monitor to know who that grating voice belonged to. "Just a sec, Mark."

Didn't matter that it was Shane's first week at the most prestigious international law firm in Sydney, Australia. Or that he was in the middle of reviewing an asset purchase agreement for a partner he wanted to impress. Because it wouldn't do to keep his paragon of an older brother waiting overlong.

Shane continued scanning the document, but sure enough, his office door still closed with a gentle *thunk*. No, *You look busy, I'll come back later.* No, *Sorry for interrupting.* Just an expectation that he'd drop everything because whatever Mark had to say was more important.

Suppressing a sigh, Shane glanced over to where his brother's flabby arse now rested against said door. Mark was a partner in the firm's real estate department, and Shane, unfortunately, owed his presently elevated circumstances to his brother's largesse.

The morning sunlight glinted off Mark's glasses as he stepped farther into the office. "I just wanted to check in, see how you were going."

Check up on him was more like it. But Shane pasted on a smile—one of those charming ones that usually got him what he wanted—and said, "Can't complain. I like my colleagues so far, the office has a fantastic view…" He paused then, tilting his head backward toward the panorama of Sydney Harbour and the Botanic Gardens spread out behind him. "And John Gallagher's got me working on a two hundred million dollar deal of his." *So let's wrap this up so I can get back to reviewing John's agreement, shall we?*

"John. Huh." Mark's eyebrows rose, chasing his receding hairline.

God, Shane hoped he didn't look like that when he turned thirty-five. At least he still had seven more years before he hit that particular milestone. Luckily, he'd also inherited their mother's thick, dark hair instead of their father's thinning strands. Not that Shane had anything against bald dudes—some guys really made the look work for them.

Mark removed his glasses, then brandished them at Shane for emphasis. "I guess I don't need to tell you how important it is that you stay in John's good graces if you want to succeed in the corporate department at Carter, Munroe and Hodges."

Shane wondered if his brother practiced sounding that officious. But he knew where this discussion was leading now. Maybe he could still head it off.

"Look. I know I screwed up. I shouldn't have hooked up with Brooke, but we're consenting adults, and we were both into it. Carleton's doesn't have an anti-fraternization policy, so there was no legitimate reason to make me resign."

"You still don't get it." Mark pulled a cloth out of his pocket and started polishing his lenses. "You weren't fired because Carleton's managing partner caught you sticking your tongue down his niece's throat—*in public*. You were fired because pashing the managing partner's niece—who was also a summer law clerk at your firm, I might add—demonstrated poor judgment. Extremely poor." He pointed his now-clean glasses at Shane again. "If your work at Carleton's hadn't been impeccable, I wouldn't have bothered sticking my neck out to bring you here."

The unexpected compliment surprised Shane into thinking he'd gotten off easy. But his brother wasn't done berating him.

"She was barely twenty years old, for Christ's sake. What were you even doing with a girl that young?" Mark shook his head, then tucked the cloth away and put his glasses back on. "Never mind, I don't want to know. Just keep it in your trousers here, all right, Shane? I'm not bailing you out a second time."

"Yes. Of course, Mark." Like getting canned for something so trivial wasn't enough of a learning experience. "Trust me, I will *never* hook up with a girl from work again."

Shane's computer chimed and his phone buzzed, signaling that he had a new e-mail message and hopefully a way out of this conversation. He nudged his mouse, waking up the monitor.

The subject, *FW: last night was epic!!*, sounded like something his best mate, Dave Watson, would send. Especially since last night *had* been rather epic. But why had it been forwarded...by...

His brain couldn't process what his eyes were telling him.

The sender's name was Shane, Tracy. Meaning, there was someone at the firm named Tracy Shane? Who'd received an e-mail that was probably about Shane's activities last night? No effing way. His luck couldn't possibly be that bad.

He opened the message, skipping straight over the brief note at the top of the e-mail to check the signature block. Yes, one Tracy M. Shane, Esq. apparently worked as an associate in the firm's New York City office.

With a growing sense of dread, he read Tracy's note next. "Hmph." Could've been worse.

Welcome to the firm, she'd written. *I'm sure this is just the first of many e-mails that will go astray. I'll forward yours if you forward mine?*

Tracy seemed like an alright chick. Holding his breath, Shane scanned the forwarded message. Dave asked how Shane had gotten on with that girl...told him he'd hooked up with the girl's hot friend after Shane and the girl had left the bar together...and suggested he and Shane get together tomorrow afternoon to celebrate—again—Shane's first week at the firm.

He winced. Dave really, really needed to be more discreet.

And Shane's brother really, really needed to be nowhere near here, so Shane could sort something out with Tracy and tell Dave to stop being a dickhead—not that accomplishing the latter would ever be possible. "Ah, Mark? I need to deal with this e-mail."

Mark opened the door but lingered in Shane's

doorway. "You coming over tomorrow? Mum and Dad will be there, and I was going to throw some lamb on the barbie, a few snags for the kids..."

Sounded like hell—incessant badgering about how he wasn't living up to his potential interspersed with fawning over Mark's perfect family. "Nah, I've got something on. But thanks."

"Suit yourself," Mark said. Though it was clear Shane's dismissive answer hadn't suited his brother at all.

Another e-mail came through then. "See ya later," Shane said, then turned back to his monitor. This message was also from Shane, Tracy.

The subject? *FW: You were incredible last night.*

He swallowed hard, trying to keep his breakfast from making a reappearance. Shane knew who this e-mail had to be from. No matter what it said, with a subject like that, it couldn't be good.

"Later," Mark said. Then his footsteps shuffled away down the corridor. Thank Christ.

Shane took a deep breath, then exhaled in a rush, hoping to settle his churning stomach. Time to find out if he was going to get fired from the second job in as many weeks.

He opened the message. But all the mysterious Tracy Shane had to say this time was, *You might consider a Gmail account. Just a thought.*

A sick sense of relief flooded him, then the heat of embarrassment swept across his face. Accompanied by a chuckle. She had a wry sense of humor, this Tracy Shane did.

The forwarded e-mail was, of course, from the girl

he'd left the bar with last night. They'd met at a networking mixer earlier in the evening, then joined a smaller group that had gone for drinks down on Circular Quay after the official event had ended. Hooking up with her afterward had been an unexpected and welcome bonus. Until she'd sent a racy morning-after e-mail *to the wrong person*.

Was it really so hard to understand that his e-mail address was tracy.shane and not the other way 'round? It must be, since two people had already messed it up. He would definitely use a personal e-mail address for all non-work e-mails from here on out, to avoid the risk of this ever happening again.

From his Hotmail account, he fired off a message to Dave. And he ignored the e-mail from last night's folly. Plausible deniability, right?

He *should* get back to reviewing the asset purchase agreement. Unwanted conversations with his brother and reading humiliating misdirected personal e-mails couldn't be billed to clients. Nor did they help him wow the partners. But he could spare a few more minutes to indulge his curiosity about Tracy M. Shane, Esq. He owed her a reply, anyway.

Since she was an associate—as opposed to a paralegal or administrative staffer—her headshot and bio were included on the firm's website. And she was... Even with her arms folded across her chest in one of those ridiculous corporate headshot poses, she was a knockout.

Glossy hair tumbled over her shoulders, a warmer shade of brown than Shane's own. And her confident smile undoubtedly appealed to her clients as much as it did to Shane. But what he found himself coming back to again and again were her remarkable eyes, as if he had to keep making sure her irises really were that unusual pale golden-green, ringed by dark gray.

Her bio was equally remarkable. She'd graduated from University of Chicago law school five years ago, and with honors from Harvard three years before that, which would make her, what…thirty? She didn't look thirty, but he supposed her picture could have been taken when she'd joined the firm, fresh out of law school. Or maybe it was just that Americans tended to look a few years younger than their Australian counterparts, who spent more time in the sun. Shane's years of surfing and playing rugby at uni had already given him crows' feet and a tan that faded during the winter, but never completely disappeared.

Like Shane, Tracy was in CMH's corporate department. Her areas of specialization were exactly the sorts of things he wanted to do—M&A, complex cross-border transactions, other cool-sounding stuff. And not in a relative backwater like Sydney. In New frickin' York, the financial capital of the world.

The way his luck was going, he'd probably end up working on a deal with her. And after receiving those two stray e-mails, she'd probably already written him off as a partier and an idiot. At best. *Nice going, arsehole.*

Or maybe his luck would improve, and they'd never meet in person. He could always hope.

In the meantime, he'd thank her for forwarding his e-mails, and he'd pretend for as long as he could that he still had a few shreds of dignity left. The truth was, he couldn't afford another screw-up. Or he'd end up as a small town lawyer out in Cowra, and his dreams of leaving Sydney behind to work on billion dollar deals would be history.

Want to be notified when *An International Affair* is available? Sign up for Alexa's low-volume newsletter at http://alexarowan.com/news, and you'll be the first to know!

ABOUT THE AUTHOR

An attorney by day, Alexa Rowan squeezes in as much writing time as she can for her steamy, intelligent contemporary and paranormal romances. Alexa is the author of the sizzling-hot BigLaw Romance series, which features smart, ambitious heroes and heroines struggling with realistic conflicts as they seek love, success, and that elusive work-life balance. *Winning Her Over* won the Romance Writers of America's prestigious Golden Heart® award for Best Short Contemporary Romance in 2015.

Alexa lives in a leafy New England suburb with her husband, two energetic children, five backyard chickens, a dumb but adorable cairn terrier, and a female leopard gecko named Fred. She also enjoys hiking and is an avid romance reader.

You can connect with Alexa by:

Signing up for Alexa's low-volume newsletter
www.alexarowan.com/news

Liking Alexa on Facebook
www.facebook.com/alexa.rowan.books

Following Alexa on Twitter
www.twitter.com/alexa_rowan